MW01255120

TANTRUM

PART I

Temper

TANTRUM

For Daniel Matthew Meiser,
LittleWing, and the WildeBeast—
my brilliant and beautiful deviants

PUTNAM
— EST. 1838 —

G. P. PUTNAM'S SONS
Publishers Since 1838
An imprint of Penguin Random House LLC
1745 Broadway, New York, NY 10019
penguinrandomhouse.com

Copyright © 2025 by Rachel Eve Moulton
Penguin Random House values and supports copyright.
Copyright fuels creativity, encourages diverse voices, promotes free speech, and creates
a vibrant culture. Thank you for buying an authorized edition of this book and for
complying with copyright laws by not reproducing, scanning, or distributing any part
of it in any form without permission. You are supporting writers and allowing
Penguin Random House to continue to publish books for every reader.
Please note that no part of this book may be used or reproduced in any manner
for the purpose of training artificial intelligence technologies or systems.

Book design by Laura K. Corless

Library of Congress Cataloging-in-Publication Data

Names: Moulton, Rachel Eve, 1975– author.
Title: Tantrum / Rachel Eve Moulton.
Description: New York: G. P. Putnam's Sons, 2025.
Identifiers: LCCN 2024033344 (print) | LCCN 2024033345 (ebook) |
ISBN 9780593854600 (hardcover) | ISBN 9780593854617 (epub)
Subjects: LCGFT: Horror fiction. | Novellas.
Classification: LCC PS3613.O854 C37 2025 (print) | LCC PS3613.O854 (ebook) |
DDC 813/.6—dc23/eng/20240719
LC record available at https://lccn.loc.gov/2024033344
LC ebook record available at https://lccn.loc.gov/2024033345

Printed in the United States of America
1st Printing

The authorized representative in the EU for product safety and compliance is
Penguin Random House Ireland, Morrison Chambers, 32 Nassau Street,
Dublin D02 YH68, Ireland, https://eu-contact.penguin.ie.

TANTRUM

RACHEL EVE MOULTON

G. P. PUTNAM'S SONS
NEW YORK

I extricate Lucia from her high chair, throw a bath towel over my shoulder, and grab a basket for the eggs that I hope to collect, all with Lucia held tightly on my hip.

"Sit right here," I say to Lucia as I lay the towel on the ground next to the gate. This way Lucia can watch me pick up eggs but can't enter the coop, where she might grab a handful of chicken poop, and I can pretend I'm getting a moment to myself. Lucia sits primly on the ground with her head held high, her shoulders back, and her spine straight in a posture no three-month-old should have while I wiggle open the high gate my husband built for us from chicken wire and spare wood.

The coyotes made a bloody mess of things before we made the fence taller. Dillon had to dig it a foot deep to keep them from going under. Coyotes are scruffy out here, hungry from heat. Like rattlesnakes and scorpions, they are not to be messed with. We lost a lot of chickens that first year, and I will admit, each loss broke my heart a little. I'd raised them from chicks and given them my favorite dastardly names—female villains are an obsession of mine.

This morning I'm immediately greeted by the fabulous Alex Forrest—a chicken that boasts Glenn Close's high curly locks from *Fatal Attraction*. She's a spirited chicken. Certain of what she wants. We had a rooster for a while, named after Michael Douglas's character—I was secretly pleased when coyotes picked Dan Gallagher off.

"Morning, Alex," I say, genuinely glad for her plucky, persis-

forgot to gather the chicken eggs first thing this morning. It's what I'm supposed to do after I do all my other firsts—change diapers, start coffee, put on underwear (clean preferred but not necessary), pour cereal, cut fruit, smell own armpits, and wipe down all three children. If I do all this efficiently, I earn five minutes outside in the morning air by myself in the chicken coop. Today, Sebastian's blowout means I'm not so lucky. You've never managed shit until you've had children shoot it up their own back, crack to head.

I try motioning to my husband, Dillon, asking him to watch Lucia while I go outside. He is at one end of the kitchen table; she is at the other in her high chair. It isn't a big favor, but he shakes his head no and gestures to the little squares of people on his laptop screen. Among the more surprising things about parenthood is how much of a throwback it is to when you were a preteen and had to ask your parents' permission to do just about anything. Or, even harsher but perhaps more apt, it's what I imagine it must be like to serve some light jail time. Permission must be obtained to exit your cell, shower, take a piss, call a friend. It turns out too, that being the breadwinner allows a bit of leniency—guess I shouldn't have stopped earning money.

tent self. Mystique and Regina George strut over to join us. I sprinkle food, and the rest of the chickens plunder out of their coop so that I can lift the roof and reach in. The eggs are warm and almost soft to the touch. One speckled brown egg fills my palm, and there is something so beautiful about it. You aren't supposed to gather eggs or even go into the chicken coop when you're pregnant, but I did it anyway with Lucia. After carrying and giving birth to two boys, I was done being careful and had stood, twelve weeks pregnant and holding a chicken egg in my hand, thinking, *My baby is this big today.* It was a sweet moment, a sweet thought, until Lucia was born.

Gathering the eggs always reminds me that things can be simple. I'm feeling that good, whole feeling of being in the world that is rare for me when I hear a mad squawking.

I let the roof of the chicken coop slam shut and spin on my heels.

"Lucia!" I shriek. I drop my egg basket. She's got Alex's head pulled through the tight weave of the mesh. "Stop that! You're hurting her!"

Lucia does not stop. Lucia giggles and twists.

I head straight for the gate, opening and shutting it behind me, but I'm too late. Lucia has Alex Forrest's head in her hand. She sits at the edge of the fence coated in blood, laughing that full-bellied baby laugh that we loved so much when the boys were infants. Lucia's laugh, as with all things Lucia, is tinged with a glee that feels targeted. Is she laughing with us or at us?

She shouldn't have the dexterity to wrap both hands around a chicken neck, let alone to pull apart the mesh and create a large enough hole to coax the stupid creature through in the first place. She smiles at me from atop her towel, a chicken head still clutched in her pudgy little hands.

"Lucia," I say sternly. "Why would you do that?"

Lucia holds the head up proudly for me to see. I watch as she attempts to shove the whole of her free hand into the bloody mess of the poor chicken's severed neck. It's a horrifying spectacle, and almost as if she thinks the severed head is a doll she can manipulate, a ventriloquist's dummy whose beak will soon be spitting out inane jokes if she has her way. I swallow hard, holding back the instinctive urge to vomit. I look away from my daughter to see that the rest of Alex Forrest is still on the other side of the fence. A bloody blond body thrashing on the ground, blood spraying from the neck.

Frozen, my heart races. I look at the chicken wire, at the tiny hexagonal pattern of the fence and the hole she has made to pull the chicken head through.

"How is that even possible?" I ask her. The other chickens have stopped eating. They watch their sister's feet try to gain a headless purchase and fail. The dirt of the coop reddens. "Fuck me," I say.

What do I do first? A normal mother would grab her child. Get the decapitated head away from her and take her inside to bathe off the blood. But a normal mother of a normal child wouldn't stand and watch her daughter play with said head in the first place.

I leave her to her puppeteering and reenter the coop. I pick up the body quickly, bravely I think, and throw it over the other edge of the fence. A talon scratches me from the inside of my elbow to the wrist. Blood pools. I ignore it. My blood is nothing compared to the gush of this one hot chicken.

I let myself back out and swoop up my bloody baby. I snatch the head away from her and hurl it across the top of the coop. I intend it to land near its body on the other side, but of course, it doesn't. It plops at the scaly, yellow feet of the rest of the chickens, and I turn to the house before I can see their reactions—running in tight circles with their wings flapping, beaks pointed upward to their chicken god as they scream in a useless, squawking panic.

"Everything okay?" Dillon asks alarmed, but I can see he has only muted his meeting, not turned off the camera, so he rushes and fumbles to hide the murder scene that is this family.

"Fine," I say, clearly not fine.

"Mama," Jeremy says. "Blood?"

"Blood!" Sebastian yells in joyful mimicry of his brother.

"It's not ours!" I shout. "We lost Alex Forrest."

"Coyote?" Dillon asks as I shut and lock the bathroom door.

"Sure," I say through the door.

"Honey, what's going on?" I can tell that he's stressed, that he's got his mouth pressed to the other side of the door, so the boys don't hear his worry.

"Don't worry. We're fine. Promise." I raise the pitch of my voice to try to convince him just how fine we are.

"Do you need help?" he asks.

Dillon wants to help me. Why won't I let him help me? It's a bad habit of mine, not letting people help. It comes right after my first and worst habit of safely assuming they won't notice that I need help in the first place or, even if they do, that they won't offer it or will offer it but not actually mean it. The problems of other people are, after all, a massive inconvenience. Who would ever disagree with that statement? I've found it's best to function as independently from others as possible, so as not to be disappointed or taken by surprise by someone else's lack of care for you. My life—childhood up until Lucia's birth—was a self-imposed proving ground that I am out here all on my own.

"I got it," I say. "Go back to work."

"Make sure she doesn't ingest any of that . . ."

"Blood," I say for him. "Sure thing."

I put Lucia in the bathtub. I sit on the lid of the toilet and watch her lick her fingers as if they are Popsicles.

˅ ˅

With Lucia clean and me as clean as I'll ever be, I head out of our bathroom and back into the noise of the living room/kitchen with Lucia heavy in my arms.

Sebastian and Jeremy are playing "frucks"—this is what

Sebastian calls any truck or vehicle, which is super cute until we're in public. They like to vroom them around the floor, using swirls in the stained concrete to create highways.

Dillon has shut his laptop, but he's standing up with his cell held to his ear. Seeing Lucia and me emerge from the bathroom, he quickly hangs up.

"Who was that?" I ask. The guilt on his face lets me know it wasn't a work call.

"Are my girls okay?" he asks, avoiding my question. "I was worried."

I need to head out on my daily morning walk before it gets too hot, but Sebastian is still in his sleepy diaper—it's just a nighttime pull-up, but we've accidentally personified it for him, so now he thinks his diaper is just as sleepy at night as he is—and I need more coffee. I always need more coffee.

"Can Lucia play with you two?" I ask.

I've noticed Jeremy, now five, has become wary of Lucia, although I don't know specifically why or when the wariness started. He's careful around her and not in the way he was right after she came home from the hospital—in that big brother way that one hopes to see in their son—but as if he's keeping his distance and sometimes even inserting his body between two-year-old Sebastian and her. I've tried to ask him. Inquire in a way that I hope sounds casual, but Jeremy is tight-lipped on the subject.

Perhaps she already tried a little head-ripping on her big brother

— 9 —

before she got to Alex Forrest, I think to myself. My brain is trying to make light of the situation, but even as a private joke that no one will ever know I told, it doesn't land. A shiver goes up and down my spine. I focus on sweet Sebastian, who, right or wrong, still adores his baby sister.

"Yes, pease! Play with us," Sebastian answers with his usual cheer.

Dillon and I decided on three children from the start, before we knew who any of them would be, and our first two are, by all measures, perfect. And I'm not just saying that because I'm their mother. They are handsome, active, kind, and clever. They hit their benchmarks right on time—not too soon and not too late. Of course, I've spent the last three months protecting them and my husband from our third baby, who, in all likelihood, is some kind of devil. I hope they'll forgive me for not only allowing this chunky piece of dynamite into their lives, but for making it fat with maliciousness before I ever pushed it out of my ravaged lady parts.

I pour myself a coffee, using the mug I hadn't quite drained before the bloodletting. The result is a lukewarm brew, but I sip it anyway. We don't own a microwave—it's some misplaced virtue signaling of Dillon's based either on the idea that such devices will give you cancer or on the simple righteousness that nuked food is not healthy for kids but rather stripped of nutrients during its one-minute spin around a modest glass turntable. Sometimes—no, always—I want to be less *Little House on the*

Prairie and more standard American. I don't tell Dillon this. He is far too proud of what he's built for me to complain.

Lucia, still held to my side with the hand not clutching my coffee, claps at her brothers as they make their honks and beeps and crashing noises louder and louder.

"Lucia!" Dillon exclaims. He claps his hands back at her as he makes his way over to us and eases her out of my grasp. With her weight gone, I feel lighter, if only for a second. "Come play with your brothers."

Dillon sets her in her bouncy chair and straps her in so she can be closer to them. I resist the urge to tell him she doesn't need it: *Might as well set the murderous creature right on the damn floor.* Dillon plops on the ground to play with them. He revs their little cars around in tight circles with a full-throated commitment. He's good at meeting them at their level both literally and figuratively. He makes eye contact when he speaks with them and listens to their ideas—it's a small thing, listening, that surprisingly few adults do.

I lean back on the edge of the kitchen sink and watch my family play and wonder what it might have been like to have grown up with a father and a good one at that. Mine fled the scene so fast that it's sometimes hard to believe my mother even used a man to make me. A part of me will always believe that she brewed me up out of her own loneliness—no egg or sperm required—a child she dubbed her best friend, because no one else would have her or because she would have no one else. And, while I was often good to her or for her, listened to her ailments and rubbed her back when she was too depressed to get out of bed, I realized early in my adulthood that she only really showed an interest in me when she was between men and sober enough to get off the couch. I may have been her best friend, but she was never mine.

I watch Dillon ruffle Jeremy's hair and admire how Jeremy tilts his body into Dillon's. The full weight of his little boy love and trust resting on his daddy's shoulder. Sometimes I'm jealous of my children—a feeling that I'm sure will send me straight to hell—then I remember that they have me for a mother and life will never be quite as good as they deserve.

Jealousy isn't the only unmotherly feeling I have about my children. First, and more so today than ever, I harbor an intense fear of my daughter that I haven't had the guts to tell anyone about. I'm scared of Lucia, although I haven't confessed this to my husband, nor to my husband's parents, and certainly not to my own mother. I haven't even told my friends over multiple Zoom calls, but surely this morning's decapitation signals it's time to tell someone. To ask, at least, if it's just me who has noticed how freakishly strong her neck is or how she uses that powerful little swizzle stick to swish her head back and forth, following every conversation like a dog follows a tennis ball.

"I'll be right back," I say and head swiftly back to the haven of my bathroom, coffee still in hand.

I lock the door, sit on the toilet (lid closed), and scroll through my contacts.

Honestly, even pre–chicken decapitation, Lucia scared the shit out of me. She has since the day she was born. And it makes sense, after all, that my third baby, my only girl, was born with a little something extra going on. I've got forty-two-year-old eggs that barely make the effort to shed themselves every month and probably bake up translucent when they bother to bake up at all. They've got no red left to them, no special life-giving goo. Those bloodless little fuckers are probably holding on to the shittiest bits of my genetics right now, so we are relying on my husband's sweet little tapioca-baby-boba swimmers, and those come from a long line of emotionally stunted auto mechanics. But none of these factors explain *her*. Honest to fucking God, I'd rather she had devil horns, a forked tail or tongue, or maybe even furry legs and cloven hooves. Something I could point at to prove what I think about her has merit. Anything that would, at the very least, let me confess to my innumerable parade of doctors—pediatrician, gyno, primary care, chiropractor, podiatrist, dentist, marriage counselor, random urgent care bitch—that this kid is not right.

Suddenly the answer to who to call is obvious. I'm surprised I haven't already done it. Tori. My doula. I'll call the woman who helped deliver Lucia. She's used to pregnant women and new mothers asking her batshit questions—she's surely heard it all. Well, maybe not this, but I can tell her anything. Maybe even that Lucia killed a chicken this morning with her bare hands.

The phone rings, and with my big toe I push at the multicolored rag rug we keep in front of the bathroom sink. My toenails

are far too long, scraggly even, and I feel instantly disgusted with myself. I pull the rug a bit closer to try to cover my gnarly feet before realizing how badly the rug needs to be washed. When was the last time I cleaned it? And the bath towels? I can smell them mildewing even from this distance and look to see that our hand towel is speckled stiff with God knows what. The heaviness of all I've been neglecting makes me slump lower on the toilet as the phone rings and rings.

I wonder briefly if Tori is done with me now that we're no longer paying her to care. Or, maybe, and more likely, she's off somewhere delivering someone else's kid. A sweet little girl named Lily or Ivy or Rose. I picture my doula leaning over some other woman's birthing tub, massaging some other woman's shoulders, and I feel that nasty pang of jealousy again.

What a shit person I am, I think just as Tori finally picks up.

"Thea!" she shouts into the line, as if I'm just the woman she's been waiting to talk to. "How are you, sweetheart? How are your darling babies? How old is Jeremy now? Is Sebastian walking?"

It's too many questions all at once, and I don't know what to answer first, so I don't answer any of them. Instead, I say, "Sorry to bother you, Tori."

"You've never been a bother," she says, and I can hear her metal bracelets banging together. I picture her in one of her many flowing, floral skirts with her signature black leggings underneath. Those bracelets and that skirt came right off during delivery. She was all business in her tank top and yoga tights.

Even her mass of graying, curly hair was suddenly and unimaginably tamed. "Tell me. What's going on with you?"

Her voice is so kind. Is this what she always sounds like? My eyes well up with tears.

"I'm doing great, actually," I say, lying. "The boys are thriving. Sebastian is as good-natured as the day he was born."

She waits for me to say something about Lucia. I let the silence go too long.

"And how is your baby girl? Is she holding her weight?"

"Oh, yes, and then some." I laugh.

A tear spills out of my right eye and down my cheek. I swipe it away angrily.

"Breastfeeding is a miracle, isn't it?" Tori asks, but she isn't really asking. She's basking in the glow of her own good advice and something in me begins to shut down, dry up. I don't have the heart to tell her I stopped breastfeeding Lucia weeks ago for fear of losing a nipple. Or how Dillon thought it briefly funny to nickname her Jaws until my death stare made him stop. "How is *your* body, Thea? I know pregnancy wasn't your favorite state of being. Do you feel more yourself these days?"

Getting a doula for Lucia, our third and final child, was Dillon's idea. He found Tori on the internet and hired her before I could say no. He couched it as a birthday present, making the idea impossible to turn down. We hadn't used a doula for Jeremy or Sebastian, but I suppose my husband remembered my fear leading up to the births of my two sons.

"I'm healing. Almost all the way there," I say. "I guess I'm just bad at being pregnant."

"Oh, nonsense. You did an excellent job!"

I had myself convinced when I was pregnant with our first two that something was wrong with them. I thought they'd be born green with black holes for eyes or have tentacles sprouting from their torsos complete with a million little suction cups. With Lucia, however, I no longer worried. I'd learned my lesson. I was pregnant with a baby and would birth a baby. I had no doubt she was normal and fine. I tried to tell Dillon this. To explain that extra help was not necessary. Jeremy, after all, came out smart and curious. Sebastian came out laughing. Glee is his predominant emotion. We didn't need a doula. Hands off is my preferred state of things, so I didn't lean on Tori at all until I was at ten centimeters, and the suffering was at its most extreme. At that point, I would have taken any relief I could get.

"I did okay, I guess," I say. It's true that I gave up alcohol and kept up with some form of exercise during all three pregnancies. I'd read up on child-rearing—hell, there was still a stack of books on my bedside table that might cause a concussion if it tumbled onto a small head. "Do you think I should have done anything different with Lucia? Maybe my body needed something different because it was making a girl?"

"Where is this coming from?" Tori asks.

I can hear her two kids arguing softly in the background. I shouldn't be bothering her.

"I just felt so monstrous when I was pregnant, and I was so careful with the boys. I did everything right with them, but with Lucia, I got lazy."

"Lazy, how?"

"I don't know," I say. "I ate soft cheeses. I drank caffeine." I sound so fucking stupid. The truth of what I want to say is stuck in my throat. I feel like I will choke on it.

"Is Lucia healthy?"

"I guess so," I say, because she is *physically* healthy. Freakishly so.

"There is not one way to be pregnant, Thea. Just like there isn't one way to be a good mom. Some women I work with love pregnancy, but others truly hate it. You were somewhere in the middle with Lucia, I'd say, which is perfectly normal," Tori says.

"Okay," I say meekly.

I have never understood which woman could possibly love being pregnant. Your body is invaded by alien beings. The signs of devilishness are evident and everywhere! My thighs became their own chunky creatures. They rubbed against each other on the smallest of walks, say from the stove to the trash bin. Or the trash bin to the garage. *Rub, rub, rub.* Creating a hot little friction that carried no pleasure with it, just two little, red, raw patches. I had to walk around like I'd just jumped off a horse. On top of that not-so-small indignity, I ate mercilessly with Lucia. Entire jars of sugary peanut butter or the twenty-packs of nuggets from that bigoted chicken place. My body couldn't get

— 17 —

enough poison—grease, fat, salt, those big chewy tarts that come in packs of four. It's probably exactly why Lucia turned out the way she did. If my heart burned so hot every evening that bile would come right up my throat and sit at the back of my tongue, what must it have been doing to her tiny fetal heart?

I didn't even want children until I met Dillon. I didn't want any of this. Not the isolation, the endless hours of each day with no start or conclusion, or the dusty roads. I was a fucking film-maker for God's sake, climbing the ladder slow and steady, and now our internet barely works. I live in the high desert—off the grid in a house my husband built from hay and mud—and I have goats for neighbors.

"Are you menstruating yet?"

"Excuse me?"

"Did your period come back?"

Now that my body is no longer under siege of birth, the question feels invasive. I want to ask: *No, how about you? Are you bleeding right now?* I remind myself that I called her, and this is her job of choice.

"Not yet."

"Okay, remember you can still get pregnant."

"Oh, we've got that handled," I say. Finally, something I'm certain of. My husband's tubes tied, his testes bundled, peanuts packed tightly away.

"Good job, Dillon. Tell him I said well done."

"I will," I say, only I know I won't. No man deserves a medal for having someone mess with his balls. He was sore for a day or two. Sore! Pregnancy alters a body for life. I still begin each day waddling.

"Thea, I have to say, you sound a bit . . . shut down. Remember, I picked up the phone to talk with you. You can tell me what's going on. Is it your mother?"

"My mother?" I ask and blink. I'm startled that she knows anything about my mother. Did they meet at the hospital? No. What had I shared? I vaguely remember crying when she asked if my mother was on her way, but had I explained my reaction? Childbirth does tend to leave a kind of pitch-black hole in one's memory. A saving grace, I suppose, and the reason any of us are willing to give birth more than once.

"I sense your mother is a source of trauma for you."

"Jesus Christ," I say, not at all meaning to say it out loud.

"Forgive me if I've overstepped."

"It's fine," I say. "Sorry to bother you today, Tori. I'll let you go."

"Thea," Tori says sternly. It's her authoritative voice and it's a good one. I bet she is an amazing mother. Her tone makes me sit up and listen. "I can't let you off the phone in good conscience if you don't tell me why you've called."

I've dug myself into a little hole.

"Lucia is . . . different. Harder than I remember the boys being."

"Fussy?"

"No."

"Does she sleep?"

"Yes."

"Is she allowing Dad to care for her?"

"Yes."

"What is it, Thea? Be specific. I've seen it all, so you can't shock me."

I laugh a cruel little laugh, thinking of how small her imagination must be compared to my reality.

"Fine, Thea, but remember, you called me. I need to hear that you're okay if you aren't going to share why you called," she says, and it's the first time I've heard exasperation in her voice.

I scramble to think of something worthy to ask of her. Something to get us both off the phone as smoothly and quickly as possible. Or, maybe, alternately, I should say something real and pressing. I should fucking spit out what I really called to confess. Something that will get Tori in her beat-up, barn-red Prius chugging up Interstate 40 to get to me as quickly as possible. Something like: *Lucia is a demon baby, and I'm pretty sure she will eventually murder her brothers and maybe me and her father too, and she's a chicken murderer so soon she will be bigger and probably prone to genocide and all of this is certainly because of how shitty I am as a mother and a sign that I probably didn't want to have a little girl at all, right? Right, Tori?*

Instead, I blurt out: "I'm not sleeping even when the baby sleeps."

"Ahhh," she says. I've done it. I've given her a topic she knows how to handle. She talks for a time about herbal remedies and exercise. She reminds me of the need for sunlight daily. She launches into a lengthy lecture on gut health. I don't listen very well, but I don't need to since none of it is about how to identify early signs of salmonella poisoning in a child who has recently digested an excessive amount of chicken blood.

"Listen," she's saying. "We both know that the twelve weeks after the baby is born is in some ways the most difficult, now you're hitting the end of that 'fourth trimester.' The baby is better able to live outside the womb, and it all becomes more manageable. Of course, there is also *your* recovery from childbirth to consider. It takes a toll even when all goes well. Bleeding and general wound recovery, chronic exhaustion, hair loss, breast pain. Thoughts of self-harm. Are you having any?"

My brain is still stuck on the phrase "general wound recovery," and its use as a euphemism for the abysmal state of my vagina, so I don't answer her question straightaway. My delay further alarms her.

"Are you having thoughts of self-harm?" Tori repeats.

"No. Of course not." I hear the defensiveness in my own voice, but I can't stop it.

I'm thinking of a week prior when I left the refrigerator door open while I prepped dinner. At some point, I turned around to see Lucia at the base of the fridge with raw bacon strips clenched in both fists like fatty pink-and-red bunches of heavily wilted flowers. The sheen around her mouth told me she'd already consumed a healthy chunk of raw pork, and her grin told me she was proud of herself and ready to eat more.

"Any thoughts of harming the baby?" she asks.

"Hardly." I snort. "She's more likely to harm me," I mumble.

"Oh, shoot, I'm getting another call, likely about a birthing. A brand-new mama!" Tori's joy is back. Her love for her work in full force. "I need to answer, but I'll check on you in a few days."

"Okay, thanks," I say sullenly, already disappointed in myself for being such a coward.

"Oh! I forgot to mention. I have another new mom who went to this spa place that turns out to be right by you. She says the woman who owns it is incredible. A former therapist, I think. She does sound baths and everything. Do you know her?"

"Lilibeth," I say flatly. I know Lilibeth well—or as well as I intend to. She is, in fact, my nosy neighbor, who chronically invites us over. She refers to herself as a "recovered psychoanalyst," yet she is awfully happy to ask endless questions and offer unsolicited advice. She may have once been a good therapist, but she's a shitty neighbor. "She's too new age for me."

"I can understand that, but sometimes you have to use the resources you're handed, Thea. Accepting help is a good life skill and she's right there, practically living with you!" Tori's energy glows through my cell phone.

"She doesn't live *with* us. She's a neighbor," I say. I do realize arguing semantics about Tori's enthusiastic recommendation is ridiculous, but somehow, I can't stop myself from being grumpy now that I've entirely failed at this phone call.

"Promise me you'll think on asking her for help."

"Ummm," I say, not getting anything else out before Tori is gleefully shouting into the receiver again.

"Must go, my love, but I'm holding you in the light. Kisses to the babies!" she practically shouts at me, then she's gone. Gone.

I sit alone on the toilet. My mind blank and my coffee now frigid. My phone buzzes again in my hand and for a moment I am ecstatic. I almost answer, thinking with a rush of love that it is Tori calling back to give me a second chance to speak the truth, to ask for help. Instead, my caller ID reads: **Text Stop to Opt Out.** It's my mother. Dillon changed her caller ID to make me laugh. It worked the first few times, and once I even hung up on her only to text her the word: **STOP.** She childishly texted back: **You STOP.** I don't think she was being silly or self-aware. The whole caller ID thing got less funny after that, but I still haven't changed it.

I silence my mother's call, dump my coffee down the sink, and flush the toilet before exiting the bathroom.

⌄ ⌄

My mother just called," I tell Dillon.
"What did she say?" he asks. He's made little snack plates for the kids and his mouth is full of baby carrots.

"I didn't answer."

"Why not?"

"Why would I?"

Dillon shrugs.

"I have to get out on my walk if I don't want it to get too hot out there. It's almost too late as it is."

"Fine by me, but your mother will keep calling until she gets you. Sometimes it's better to just deal with her straightaway."

"What the hell is that supposed to mean?" I ask.

He holds up his hands in surrender. "Nothing, Thea. Just trying to help." He puts another carrot in his mouth, and that first crunch and the excessive chewing that follows makes me want to punch him in the face.

Before I met my husband at the Dirty Bourbon, I was living in Nob Hill working in film and building myself up on social media with the hope of someday starting my own production company. It was naïve—I know that now. I come from poverty and any money I have is hard earned. A producer needs cash. Connections. I come by neither of these things plentifully or naturally. I was also drinking too much and sleeping with men I didn't want to see in the daylight. I suppose I was trying to drown out the noise of my past, which was somehow only getting louder and louder. I was working a ton—the film industry in New Mexico is booming—but it was also, strangely, the first time I hadn't been reaching for the next thing. I'd earned my BA, then my MFA. I owned a house. I had steady income. I had a career. Why wasn't I happy?

There were so many signs that I was fine. Or should have been. I wasn't my mother. I didn't need a man or a family. I only needed myself. I'd paid my deposit for my house on Carlisle, leaving a modest mortgage that I could handle. A petite Pueblo revival with a bright red front door. I was a city girl before my ovaries started talking to me and I saw Dillon seeing me on the dance floor. Some eclectic New Orleans band was playing, and I was doing shots. Dillon isn't much taller than me, but he's got a full head of dark hair and big broad shoulders. His T-shirt stretched tight over his chest. I was easy pickings despite my success and happiness and general resolve to continue being successful and happy. Now I live off the grid in the East Mountains, and every morning I wake up wondering why I've trapped myself in this hellish loop of motherhood and marital bliss.

It wasn't just the hormones that got me. It was Dillon. His easy confidence. His certainty that what he was building was a forever home. He had a college degree, a steady job, a big patch of land, and a desire for three to four children. I liked the idea of him. Of the land. It was self-destructive, but when you give up drinking for love and babies, people tend not to object. They congratulate you. Tell you how envious they are. They help you sell your house. "You found a good one," they say with a dreamy look, as if I've hit three cherries at the casino. As if marriage is the end of a story and not just the boring-ass beginning. Especially when you're going on forty or will be by the time you get out the first two babies.

When I first met Dillon, I assumed he was a cowboy—with his boots and hat and his massive family. His swath of land sealed the image in my mind, and so I let him think he could wrangle me, break me. I let him bring me here and fill me up. I asked him to do so, of course, but only a man would be blind to my true self. Only a man pretending to be a cowboy would think he could break a monster like me.

I find my hiking shoes, dust-covered from yesterday's walk, and realize I still need socks. I head into our bedroom to find a good pair, yelling over my shoulder, "Please get Sebastian ready!"

"I can't, honey," Dillon says back. I hate it when he calls me "honey," mostly because it often happens when he isn't feeling at all affectionately toward me. It's a placeholder for him, a word to get us through to the next moment without conflict. "I'm about to hop on a call again. Sorry."

I sigh too heavily, so he will hear it, and slam my dresser drawer. Socks now in hand, I plop down on the edge of the bed to put them on. When did I become so passive-aggressive? Maybe it comes naturally with motherhood, especially if motherhood doesn't come naturally.

I knew with my first pregnancy that I'd bitten off more than I could chew. I was lonely out here in the middle of nothing. Bored out of my fucking mind. Plus, there wasn't a day I didn't want my body back. The very fact that this whole process of family-making requires a woman to onboard a roommate who will literally eat her energy while the man saunters on with his average day still makes me feel sick. And yet, I'm a practical person. I knew if I wanted a family, someone with a uterus—me—would have to carry the babies all the way up until D-Day—when you'll be so excited to get normal-size fingers and ankles back that you won't care your vagina is being ripped open by a presumably human skull.

It's super sexy. The whole process. Start to finish sexy.

My mother warned me. She warned me over and over again when I was growing up that a baby ruins a body, so my resolution to never have kids happened early in the fitting room of a Gap at the Coronado Mall.

v v

I'm fourteen, about to enter high school, and my body feels like a hot rash of alien parts that excrete and expand and threaten to reproduce without warning. It's all a big bloody mess that I try to cover up as much as possible to cut down on the commentary made unprompted by just about anyone—boys at school, acquaintances, friends, the entirety of the male homeless population in Albuquerque, my mother.

Today, I certainly would have preferred privacy. My mother could have asked if I wanted her in the fitting room with me, or she could have stayed outside. Instead, she walks in first and settles right into the little white chair in the corner. Asking her to leave would mean hurting her feelings, so I adjust, distance myself from my body.

There is one of those stickers that they put on the crotches of unsold bathing suits stuck to the wall. It reads: For Hygienic Purposes. Do Not Remove. Maintain Personal Coverage. It sits like a bow tie right above my mother's head, and I feel its disappointment in me and my general inability to "maintain personal coverage."

"The light in these places is specifically designed to make you look like shit," my mother says as I take off my jeans. My legs goosepimple in the cool air.

"You look pretty, Mom," I say as I rush my legs into a pair of corduroys that won't quite button over my belly. *Fat fuck*, I think and poke at myself.

"No, I don't. Look at these wrinkles. I'm getting jowls!" She pulls at either side of her jaw until her skin does hang a bit lower. "You don't understand yet. You're still perfect. Nearly perfect, anyway. I used to have *that* body," she says, and gestures at me with a flick of her limp wrist. Does she want to be like me or rid of me? Either way I feel shame and hurry to pull off my T-shirt and slip on a blue knit dress that she picked out.

"What do you think?" I ask.

My hips dent inward in a weird way that the dress refuses to hide. Also, I don't like the way my bra shows through the fabric, creating a little mound of fat across my back.

"I wasn't flabby until after you." She slumps her shoulders lower, so her belly pooches out.

"You're beautiful, Mom. Maybe we should get *you* some clothes!" I feel like a sudden genius.

"I'm too fat," she says with a full, grim resolve I've been trying to disrupt my whole life. "Kids also make you poor. You can't afford a gym membership, not a good one anyway. And you certainly can't pay for a tummy tuck or a lift." She uses her hands to hoist her boobs higher. "Every cent goes to your kid once you're a parent."

I want to say: *When could you ever have afforded a tummy tuck? Haven't you been poor your whole life?* Instead, I say, "We don't have to buy anything today. I have plenty of clothes."

"Of course we have to," my mother says and reaches out to grab the tag under my armpit. She looks at the price, and I feel the little bit of plastic attached to the tag on the inside of the dress dig into my flesh. I think of that story about the princess who sleeps on top of like, a hundred mattresses but can still feel the green pea down underneath. Who is the villain in "The Princess and the Pea"? The pea? No, it was the queen.

"We won't get this, though. Not flattering," my mother says.

I blush and search for a pair of jeans to pull on underneath the dress before I pull it off.

"All it takes is one kid. Just wait for it."

Hans Christian Andersen's queen teaches her son that women must be perfect. Angelic in voice and body. The princess shows up a rain-drenched mess, so she can't possibly be the one . . . only she is. I watch myself in the brightly lit mirror, and all I can see is how much I hate myself already. The idea of it someday being worse is more than I can bear.

˅ ˅

My mom was raised in northern Ohio on some island that no longer exists. She talked about loneliness and humidity and iced-over winters. She told me never to leave the city and that Ohio is the kind of place where lakes catch on fire. My mother is crazy, and I hate her, but in a few ways, I listened. For a while, anyway. Don't visit Ohio (this one is easy), don't ask about the past (I learned to make this one feel easy), and don't have children (I fucked this one right up). I did listen, for a time, and swore off marriage and children until that last-minute switcheroo when my ovaries saw Dillon in a ball cap and started whispering, *Yum, yummy, yum, yum.*

My mother had exactly one child. Me. My father left the minute I was born. He took a good look at me to make sure I was what I was before he left—a parasite. A fair assessment if I do say so myself.

I head to the boys' room and find a pair of socks and a hoodie for Sebastian. The hoodie is light blue and so, so soft. I hold it to my nose and breathe in.

Sometimes Jeremy comes on our walks too, but he's too big

to carry and doesn't like being in a stroller anymore. I look at my watch and realize I'm far later getting out than I thought. It will be hot soon, and if I take Jeremy, he will slow us down long enough to sunburn.

"I'm leaving Jeremy with you today," I holler at Dillon, who is already focused on his computer. "The walk will be short anyway."

He gives me that wave away that tells me he hasn't heard anything.

I met Dillon around that same fateful time when my gynecologist casually referred to my eggs as geriatric. She had just finished rummaging around between my legs, and as she snapped off her gooey gloves, she said, "Babies?" I said, "What?" and sat up alarmed. I even dipped my head down between my legs, as if I were gonna be able to see up there myself. I thought for a heated second that she meant she'd seen some. A bunch of babies ready to hatch. She quickly added, "I'm just asking if you plan to have some, because you might want to do so soon. Clock is ticking." I wanted to say, "Clocks don't tick anymore, bitch." I didn't. I turned bright red and nodded; waiting for her to leave was the longest ten seconds of my life.

So, with Dillon, I saw no reason to hesitate—there would be no more one-night stands, no more double-bagging, and no more abortions (I've only had the one).

By thirty-seven, I was pregnant with baby one. By forty, I was pregnant with two. And, at forty-two, pregnant with three.

And my mother was right. If I wasn't geriatric before babies, I certainly am now. Saggy and soft and sleepless. It's fine, though. I tell myself it's fine. My friends tell me I should be glad I changed my mind in time because now I'm lucky. Lucky. It's a word that people use when they don't want to see the truth. When they hate themselves too much to notice any real-life misery.

My mother says I'm "lucky" because now I have three options—not just one—for who will take care of me when my "prolapsed uterus pokes its friendly face right out into your undies, and you piss yourself with every sneeze." She says this with just enough side-eye to make sure I know that she means that I need to be ready to take care of her saggy sack of a self. Last year she fell, broke her femur. The sudden onset of osteoporosis means she snaps like a damn twig if given half a chance, which is an idea that's been hard to adjust to because my whole childhood she was monstrously strong. Terrifying, really. Her hand on my upper arm could leave perfect bruised imprints in which I'd try to find her fingerprints.

"Sebastian, come here," I say, and he sticks out his bottom lip. He wants to stay with his brother and his trucks. "Want to put on your own socks?" I ask. This distracts him into a smile and a wobbly rising to walk to me.

"I do myself," he says mostly to himself. I love him so.

"Can't reach!" Jeremy is standing on tiptoe to try to reach a cup in the kitchen cupboard. He shouts as if he's said it a hundred times already and maybe he has. He's been warned not to climb up on the counters to get things, but I wish we'd just let him. I look to Dillon, but he has his AirPods in now and is back on his work call. He nods vigorously in agreement with an idea I can't hear.

I sigh again, loudly, but this time only for my own benefit, then I grab a blue plastic cup off the shelf.

I have a sudden and visceral memory of being in my small body, not too much older than Jeremy, and standing on the kitchen counter in that first hot apartment with my mother. The cupboard door open before me. Cereal boxes with their flaps open, their insides stale.

"There's no food left," I say to my mother. My toes stick to the vinyl countertop, and I like the way it feels when I peel them up then press them down and peel them back up again.

"There is plenty. Combine. We don't waste."

My mother found a full-length mirror by the dumpster and has it propped up against the kitchen table so she can look at herself. It's a date night.

I peer down, down, down into a box of nearly empty Cheerios. I count the O's at the bottom—twelve. They smell like sawdust.

Hopping down, I rinse a dirty bowl and fill it with bits and pieces. I do not tell her there is no milk. Instead, I sit on the floor and eat with my fingers, piece by piece to make it last longer.

My mother looks beautiful. Tight jeans. A white tank. She is putting in hoop earrings that are bigger than her entire ears.

"This guy has a job. He works at one of the labs, I think, so I might be out late. You'll be fine, right? You're a brave girl. Almost ten."

I nod vigorously to my bravery.

"I'll watch TV," I say.

"Good girl."

There is a spider on the wall behind my mother. It is small and brown and thoughtful.

She will keep me company tonight, I decide. I do get scared when my mother goes out at night. The TV helps, but it's still lonely and the city night noises change depending on the night of the week. There is always fighting. Always the sound of cars moving so fast that they burn black streaks into the asphalt that aren't at all scary in the daytime. But sometimes there are loud bangs and other times screaming. Once someone knocked on the door. Our door. I hid under the bed until Mom came home.

"Wicked Witch of the West!" I shout, having thought of a name for my new friend on the wall.

"Excuse me?" my mother says, and I flush red. I didn't mean to speak out loud, and I sure didn't mean to make her look at me. Not like that. Like I've interrupted an important conversation.

"Nothing," I mutter. There are Rice Krispies gummed up in my back teeth that I want to dig out but I wait until my mom looks away.

"Set yourself up a bed out here on the floor. You can sleep here. Just in case."

I nod my yes, then look at Wicked Witch and she nods too. She tells me we will be fine.

"I'll bring home leftovers for your dinner," Mom says, but I know that I'll have bologna roll-ups for dinner, because it's what we have, and if I add ketchup, that's like tomatoes, which is a healthy food, and she won't be home until too late for dinner anyway.

"Thank you, Mama," I say and wink at the Witch.

⌄ ⌄

Thank you, Mama," I hear it again like an echo, but then look down and realize it is Jeremy saying it to me. I'm holding his cup just out of his reach. I lower my hand and let him take it. "Love you," he says and steps to the sink.

"Love you too. Good job," I say.

The older my boys get, the less I understand why my mother was ever allowed to be a mother. I spent so much time alone.

My mom is a woman who is so vain and self-absorbed that she sleeps with a bandana tied around her head—chin to crown. She says it keeps her from getting old-lady jowls—a poor woman's facelift—but that doesn't explain why she made me do it too as a kid, a fact I didn't remember until Jeremy turned three and found an old blue bandana and wore it around his neck cowboy-style. The smothering discomfort of the memory washed over me. She also made me wear a foot brace at night. Two white shoes held together by a metal bar. I don't remember how many years she made me think that was normal, but I do remember that I refused to attach new shoes to it once I was in fifth grade and there was a possibility of being invited to a slumber party.

"Was I pigeon-toed as a kid?" I asked her when I was pregnant with Lucia.

"You had a lot of problems," my mother answered. Her cell phone echoing so I heard every criticism twice.

"No. Seriously. Why did I wear that brace?"

"That was a long time ago, Thea. It's a bitch to keep up with your damn kids. I did what I had to, and you should too."

"You're telling me I wore that just so you wouldn't have to worry about me walking around at night?"

"You were not an easy child."

Getting facts out of my mother is near impossible, but she is free wielding with elusive threats that leave me uneasy and deeply vulnerable and full of rage. The simmering kind that comes out suddenly and without borders—it's usually aimed at Dillon or the neighbor's loose dogs, but lately, I've aimed it more and more at the kids. I hate myself for this. I swore I wouldn't become my mother, and yet here I am, working on the inevitable.

My mother has been hinting at moving out here with us, and honestly, it's the biggest threat to my life yet—my mother moving in—far bigger than my devil daughter, because even if Lucia kills me, rips my chicken head right off my body, she will do less damage than my mother can do to me in one week. Dillon even suggested we build her a separate house right on our land in the exact spot where I told him I wanted to build a someday studio for myself, so that even if I never helped make another film, I'd have a place to create something, anything other than the children I've already made—I want a room of my own. Plus, that spot is special, and Dillon knows it better than anyone. Water is scarce here, and this land, our land, has two possible wells on it. One we already drilled for the house and a completely new one between us and Lilibeth that we haven't tapped yet but could. One natural water source is practically unheard of, and we have two! We could build a casita right on that spot. Sometimes, in the evenings, I sneak out and lie on that spot, looking up at the emerging stars. I swear the earth feels different in that spot. Cooler. It's like I can feel the water down there under all the sand and rock. It lulls me.

He brought the idea up again, a second time, saying, "We can build it for you, but still let her live there in her final years. When she's gone, it will of course be your space."

I said simply, "Shut the fuck up."

Suddenly I realize who he was on the phone with earlier when I caught him looking guilty. She called him first. *Of course* she called him first. She does want something.

I put my empty coffee cup in the sink and turn to Dillon.

"Was that my mother?" I ask at normal volume, ignoring the fact that he is on a work call.

It's his turn to sigh before he tilts his screen down and takes out one AirPod.

"Yeah. Seems like she may have broken a toe. I'll take her groceries when I head into town."

"Jesus Christ," I say. "Since when does a broken toe mean you can't get groceries? She has a cell. She can have them delivered."

"That's expensive, Thea. Look, I know she's not easy," Dillon says, "but she's old and alone. We have a responsibility to family."

"She's a fucking narcissist," I say, but I can see on his face that he doesn't believe me. "Okay, sure, she's not the billionaire kind who wins the presidency while bragging about raping women! Those are a fuckton easier to spot. But a narcissist can also make their life very, very small, getting the admiration they need from themselves and the people they've trapped in their world with them—family, most often. It was me, and now she's after you!"

"I know she's self-centered . . ." he says, letting his thoughts trail off.

"No," I say firmly. My cheeks are getting hot. "She's a horrible fucking person."

"Well, okay, that's sad," he says.

"It is sad. Really fucking sad, but that's how they get you. They lock you down because you feel sorry for them. They keep you small, because you can see their hurt, and you think you can help them fix the hurt, but they don't want to fix it. I did that my whole childhood. Into my damn twenties. I'm not doing that now. I'm not letting her trap you. Our kids! She begged for grandchildren yet has only met Lucia once. It's why she loves to say, 'Your boys don't like me,' when she's the one who ignores them."

"I hear you," he says, which I take as code for "You're too worked up."

And yet, I know it bothers him that she pays our boys no mind when we visit. Sebastian and Jeremy like to play in her front yard, where the fake grass is shaded, and they can sprinkle "gold" doubloons into its plastic reaches before "discovering" their glint and gathering them all up to begin again. They couldn't be easier, really, but they don't fawn over her or like the clothes she buys to dress them up in. She complains how little we visit, then complains how much it costs to feed us when we do. It's a lose-lose situation, and yet I still get sucked in sometimes. Her sadness is so big, so unfixable, that the only thing it can do is melt hot and sticky over anyone who comes near. My husband may see it, but he doesn't recognize it as dangerous. He hasn't spent his life trying to make things right for her.

"We won't do anything you don't want to do, Thea," he says. "But she's getting older. Something will have to be done. If building your mother a place out here is what needs to happen next, that's what we will do. It's what *I* can do for *you*," he says.

His kindness bowls me over, but it is also dangerously misplaced. Building a house for her on our land would be like inviting the vampire in. I'd be back to that little girl again. The one always scrambling to make my mother happy as she slowly drains me of whatever is left of my will to live.

"I'm going on my walk," I say and head for Sebastian.

Dillon grabs my arm. It's gentle but it stops me.

"I know she's not loving, and I know things were hard, but someday you are going to have to tell me what really happened to you when you were a kid."

His voice, his touch is so articulate and kind that my eyes well up with tears. I stop them from spilling, and I keep my eyes on Sebastian when I say, "How could it possibly matter what did or did not happen? I'm telling you she did a shit job. You know I don't remember all the gory details." Even as I say it, I feel my mother in it—she the great denier of details, of facts.

"It matters to me," he says.

One of my tears spills over.

"What if I'm just like her?" I whisper.

"Don't be ridiculous."

He's right. I'm an asshole but that doesn't make me a narcissist. I've been apologizing my whole life, reading the room, and taking other people's feelings into account. *I'm not her*, I tell myself.

"I love you," I say quietly.

He hugs me. I let him.

"I do have a work call. Is it okay if I hop back on? Do you need me to tell them we're having a family emergency?"

I tell him to take the call. I need to get outside before I've lost the opportunity for any walk at all today.

Dillon is a good man. He did not run when Jeremy was born. Nor Sebastian. Nor Lucia. If anything, he dug further into the relationship. He sank into each pregnancy with a solidarity and a thickening of his middle that I didn't even have to ask for. At least pregnancy never made me crazy enough to tell anyone that I pictured the babies inside me covered in scales, slithering out of me all tentacled arms and legs. Suckers pushing at the walls of my uterus, longing to tie themselves around my guts and poke their little bagged-up parts out my asshole.

I kept all my mental thoughts to myself back then. When the monsters finally decided to show themselves, everyone would see. No need to show my crazy in advance. My husband would scream. The nurses would run. The doctor would marvel. I even prepared a punch line for the peanut gallery. Legs splayed, monster-baby still connected by a big, flat pancake of a cord, I'd announce, "He has your mother's eyes." This would be funny because A) I'd known all along that this thing was no human baby, and yet I'd said nothing, and B) my husband's mother has an eyeball that doesn't always track. She and I don't get along— our best qualities each elusive to the other—although I will say that my ability to reproduce has grown a tolerance in her that an outsider might mistake as affection.

In any case, I delivered my first and second child stone-cold sober (or is it cold-stone?). The thing that had been torturing me from the inside out for near on a year would not have the advantage. If it came for me or my husband, I'd be right there ready to send it back to the hell from which it came.

My first came out healthy and normal as fuck, nine pounds,

one ounce when they handed him to me; I couldn't believe how gorgeous he was. How pink his cheeks. Green eyes that squinted with his startled cries. So many perfect toes and each with its own nail. I held him to my naked body and screamed right into his small, sweet face, "It's a baby! It's a baby!" I screamed so loudly that Dillon put his hand over my mouth to shush me before he apologized. Later, when things were quiet and my personal bits were all covered, he laughed at me and asked, "What did you think Jeremy was going to be?" I told him I thought he was going to be "the fucking devil," and he laughed even harder. I let him think I was joking, and I laughed at his laugh; we laughed and laughed. I'd been wrong.

Gloriously and foolishly wrong. This thing that had been stealing my food and my sleep was an angel.

With baby two, my second son, I felt the same way. I was sure he was evil until the minute I held him in my arms. I didn't holler in his face, but I was just as surprised by his perfect pink, screaming cheeks, his deep brown eyes, and his fists clenched with rage at the outrageous violence of the day. He was perfect. He was love. He was human. That was that.

So, with baby three. This baby. The worry was gone. I settled into pregnancy and soon into birth itself. Who cared. I almost enjoyed it. I ate too much on purpose and let others lift things for me. I let the house grow dirty, and I only exercised if the sun was out. I repeated the word "lucky" to myself so many times that I forgot what it meant. I ignored my insatiable cravings for spicy

foods—jalapeño poppers soaked in Tabasco sauce was at the top
of my list. I also ignored the way Lucia poked at me from the inside. It had seemed like a miracle when my boys pressed the bot-
toms of their precious little feet to my insides. We could see the
exact shape of their tiny toes above the sweet pads of their feet. I
told myself Lucia was the same, but now I look back and easily
remember the difference. The way she'd poke at me, tent my belly
from the inside with her pointer fingers, then press her full face
to my insides as if she was trying to see out. We could identify the
entirety of her nose and the smooth ridge of her forehead above
her fat cheeks. We pretended it was cute, the solid mask of her
pushing out my skin, but it wasn't. It was really fucking creepy.

Still, the overall experience of pregnancy felt great compared
to the boys. Even labor was easier. Four hours versus that first
sixteen with Jeremy and nine with Sebastian. Lucia was born
physically healthy in a hospital room just like the others, only
when they handed her to me, I knew. I fucking knew.

˅ ˅

I remember Lucia's birth well. We arrived at the hospital two
hours prior. I was happy to labor at home for the first two hours,
but when my water broke, Dillon got me in the car and sped us
down our dirt road fast enough to speed up labor.

I've been lucky in health, so childbirth is the only reason I've
spent time in this hospital. I learned from those first two times

that the hospital is a mad place that claims to heal you but generally buzzes with a mania that makes you feel worse. With Jeremy, we opted to stay a few nights for the sake of rest, and yet they woke us every hour on the hour to check our vitals or offer us food or perform some new test on the baby. This time, with our third, we've decided we will not stay any longer than we have to. And it seems my body agrees with our plan for efficiency. I'm almost fully dilated. I've passed that nine-centimeter moment when it seems air traffic control has announced: "Clear all pathways for takeoff!" I've puked up whatever was left inside of me. All that's left is to eject a baby.

The room is small, the lights are bright, and one wall is a curtain. A woman newer to her journey is alone on the other side. I try to be calm for her. To not holler or curse or be afraid. And I find it calms me. This trying to be brave for a woman I don't know. It's nice. Dillon is excited and tired. The nurses change faces every fifteen minutes. He asks each new nurse their name and tells them something about me and where I'm at. He's the cruise director for my massive ship of a body, and I love him for it.

"She's ten centimeters. Time to push," says nurse number 106 to my husband rather than me.

"I'm right here," I say, irritated.

I watch her check my chart for my name even though Dillon told her what it was when she walked in, then she is back touching me with gloved hands in places that do not want to be touched.

"This will happen fast now, Thea. We just need a few good pushes."

The sheets under me are stiff, the noise of them like paper. My toes are cold even though the rest of me is sweating. Dillon holds my left hand, and my right hand holds the edge of the bed.

I push.

The push is a relief. I remember this from last time. I focus on the love I'll feel when baby Lucia is in my arms. How much I remember that chemical connection I felt with Jeremy and Sebastian. How in my arms they were no longer alien. They were pure love. They were me. It's the best feeling in the entire world, falling in love entirely in the span of a second.

"Push!" Dillon says and so I do. I push. I breathe. I do not feel the pain.

She slips out of me whole on the second push. It's easy. Different than the first two. Like she is helping, shimmying her shoulders out of me.

Dillon sees her first. Tears in his eyes, he says, "Hello, my love." He says, "She's perfect, Thea. You did so good."

Dillon releases my hand, my shoulder. He moves to watch the nurse clean her face. She does not cry. She does not wriggle. They bring her to my skin as my husband focuses on the cord.

In my arms, she is heavy. Still and very much alive. I can feel her heartbeat through every limb of her body, her torso fiercely warm with her own life. Her neck is strong. Her breath solid. I look at her eyes for that moment of true love. She looks back at me calm as can be. Her eyes move over my face, an inspection, as if trying to identify if I am an employee in this grand grocery store she's entered. Might I point her in the direction of the coffee aisle? The tea?

While we look at each other, the room busies itself around us. The world must be made right again. Organized. Cleansed. More nurses come in—it's a teaching hospital, after all. The doctor. They go about their tasks without me. Without Lucia. As I stare down at her, my calm is disappearing. I don't feel that link I felt with the boys. I feel something else. Unnerved. Unsettled. *Afraid*.

Lucia is pink and perfect and whole, but something is wrong. I swear to God. She looks right up at me and into me and gives me a little nod of her fat-necked head. A nod that says, *'Sup*, and I drop her. My arms turn to complete jelly, and she rolls free. Luckily, Dillon is there. Right next to me to catch her so she doesn't keep rolling and slide off onto the floor.

Dillon looks horrified. He gives me a little critical scowl and holds her tighter. I don't say anything. What could I possibly say?

⌄ ⌄

As I strap Sebastian and Lucia into the double stroller, I pause to consider that maybe I should keep him separate from his geek show of a sister. I shudder despite the heat and consider my options. Sebastian is too heavy to carry for long. I won't make it down the dirt drive with him strapped to me. I could leave him home with his father, but since his dad doesn't know his sister can decapitate a chicken with her bare hands, he's likely to be irritated, as well as unable to watch Sebastian properly, which is likely more dangerous than him being with his baby sister and his mother. Right? If I let him walk, we will be out here forever. We will all end up burnt and dehydrated. In the end, I decide that Lucia hasn't ever tried to hurt her brothers, and what can she actually get done if I keep them out in front of me where I can see them through the little mesh screen.

I will say that every single person who meets Lucia marvels at her calm, her "intelligent" eyes, and her angelic beauty. They meet her and gasp, actually gasp, then say, "Wow, Thea. She looks just like you!" I've watched complete strangers look from her to me and back again. I've learned to catch the moment—the one right before their face jumps back to joy—in which I see them see the monster in her. It's a sick little *click* of a moment where I see the tip of a realization on their tongue. The tippy top of the shit I have on my hands. A beat of truth when they let themselves see the pile I've made. Like I stuck a googly eye on a dog turd. It's a blip, then it's gone.

It is, in fact, about to happen right now on my morning walk.

We live in the high desert on the greenside of the mountain so it's always ten degrees cooler than the city, but it is still essential to get out by 7:00 a.m. or the sun will be too high and hot for walking. It, unfortunately, does mean that I will probably run into one of the three neighbors that we do have—besides the goats, I mean.

A few acres down from us is a yurt. The yurt sits on more acres than the owner can count. He lives alone except for his three dogs. His dogs run wild, aggressive if they come upon another animal, and tend to steal our clothes off the line. Once recently, I ran into him at the grocery—a thirty-minute drive from our house but still a small-town market—and he yelled to me across three aisles: "Lucille brought me your underwear! You best come get it." I pretended I needed my full powers of concentration to read the contents of some natural peanut butter, but everyone knew he was talking to me.

There is an elderly woman behind us and to the north. We share a driveway. She and her now-deceased husband were once therapists in the city until they found their place out here, a kind of spa where guests come and go. She hosts yoga retreats. Mountain hikes. Spiritual meditations. She's got a saltwater pool she keeps inviting us to use.

Lilibeth, the once-upon-a-time therapist and current spa owner, claims she has no regrets about giving up her livelihood in Albuquerque. She says, "Even when my husband died, I knew I'd found my home. This desert is magical and will heal anyone who lets it. Have you ever considered the power of crystals?"

It's all I can do to keep my eyes from rolling in my head. A bunch of nonsensical, new age shit if you ask me. And it doesn't seem to keep her as happy as she claims it does. She's constantly going after ineffectual side projects and has a tendency to offer observational advice that no one has solicited with a wistful look in her eye that makes it look like she's still fantasizing about an office with a couch.

The old men out here leave me alone, which is an insulting kindness. They sense my years of fertility are over and see that my haggard stance could turn into a fight at any given moment. These old fools with their dangly testicles banging on their hot little old-man knees don't give a shit about me or my kids. Sometimes they'll talk to my husband about gardening or chickens or the fools who cut over the dirt road and start little tumbleweedy fires with their discarded cigarette butts. It's the woman that I have to watch out for. Lilibeth sees us as "kindred spirits." If I don't get out early enough for my walk, she spots me and speed walks her way to me. She does that flappy turkey-wing shit with her arms that speed walkers do, and I can tell she thinks it makes her sporty. I will say that she's incredibly fast for a lady in her sixties. I guess I can give her that.

I have my AirPods in, so I can listen to my murder podcasts and not have to engage in a conversation that will surely be absurd, and yet, here comes Mrs. Lilibeth Bryson.

When I first moved in, Mrs. Lilibeth Bryson showed up at our front door with some local honey and a carved bear holding a sign that read: HOME IS WHERE THE HEART IS. I held that stupid bear sign for forty-five minutes while she chattered on about pickleball and how to differentiate between a bull snake and a rattlesnake. I was eight months pregnant at the time and so tired

I could spit. I barely said a word, but she didn't notice. Just went on and on until I about pissed myself.

"Thea! Good morning!" she shouts. "I see you have your ear-buds on!" Obviously, she shouts more loudly, doubling down on the noise of her when she sees that my "earbuds" are, indeed, in and "on."

Still, it's fun to pretend I can't hear her. We are the only two people in the entire world according to this landscape, but I keep my gaze steady on the back wheels of my double stroller—a stroller ill-equipped for the dust and potholes of our red-dirt road. Yet, somehow, we still bought it. Unfortunately, my son sits up and pushes back the awning, so he can yell at me too.

"Stop, Mama. Stop. Say hi!" His little hand comes up and over the canvas shade. He loves everyone. And since there aren't enough people out here for all his loving, he loves Lilibeth the most.

Fuck me. I take out an AirPod. Only one.

"Morning," I say. One word seems sufficient.

"Out for your morning constitutional?"

Jesus Christ. What a fucking question.

"Yes, Dillon is working from home today, so I brought these two out for a walk."

"Gonna be a scorcher," Lilibeth says. The woman states the obvious in ways that make me want to murder.

"Yep." I move to put my AirPod back into my ear, anxious to demonstrate that her next inane question isn't important enough to be heard.

"Super windy last night," she starts in, raising her voice again. "My guests were terrified, but I kept telling them 'par for the course.'"

I love my AirPods, but they are failing me today. I send them a little apology as I take the other one out and shove them both deep into the side pocket of my yoga pants—my third pair this morning, since the first pair was covered in Sebastian shit and the second chicken blood.

"Yep."

"Tumbleweeds all over this side of the street. Caught up in the long grass, I suppose. The county mowed the left side of the road and not the right. It's a fire hazard."

"Okay," I say. The irritation in my voice full-on apparent; I'm daring her to hear it. Surely, she can hear it.

"You good?" she asks. Typical. She's making her annoying presence into something wrong with me. To be fair, I don't love this question from anyone. How are you or are you well or any number of variations are blather. The answer is obviously no. They can see I'm not good. That's why they are asking in the first place. And they aren't good. I'm not good. I quit my whole life to have and raise three kids. We moved to the mountains for a pretend peace and quiet that only makes me lonely. I don't sleep. I don't have sex. I don't have friends. What I have is a baby that smirks at me all day long like she's swallowed a toxic burp she's gonna release at any minute.

"Oh, I'm dandy," I say. My voice tightens further. "How. Are.

You?" I say each word separately, robotically, so she will note that the question is simply a mix of words that etiquette requires I offer in this particular order. I don't really care how the fuck she is.

"Oh, I'm super. No complaints. I keep myself busy since Harold died."

Harold? Fuck me if I can remember if Harold was the husband or a cat.

I nod, sigh to offer a benign condolence.

"You can't let your domestic critters out. Not even for a second. That owl was on him like that," she says and snaps her fingers. "Harold was gone in the dark."

"Sucks," I say, just because she is sniffling. At least I know Harold was the cat now, although I do have a moment of picturing her dead husband picked up by an owl, his limbs flailing as he is carted off.

"What I need to do," she continues, "is make sure we're all up on our safety protocols. Fire is the biggest danger out here and folks just don't seem to get that. I know you guys do. Dillon has always been on top of things. Plus, the coyotes are mating! Not that they're a fire hazard. Ha! No! But have you heard them at night? It's downright creepy. It's wild. They've messed all over our front yard."

Only someone like Lilibeth would ever refer to the dusty red patch of prickly pear land and tumbleweeds as a yard.

"I can't blame them," I say, feeling particularly ornery today.

"What's there to do really out here besides poop and fuck?" My son giggles at either the word *poop* or *fuck*—a good mother would know—and I offer Lilibeth a malicious grin.

Lilibeth ignores me and keeps talking. She goes on and on. I can feel the sun glaring down, burning my shoulders, the tip of my nose. Did I put on sunscreen? No. I didn't. The plan was to be out earlier when I wouldn't need sunscreen.

Sebastian suddenly howls. A loud, frustrated sound with a little pain in it, and for a minute, I think it's just the sound of my soul crying out—that's what my sweet boy is after all, my soul—to tell Lilibeth to shut the fuck up, but then the old lady is on the move. Busting into the stroller with her pale-ass old lady arms.

"Hey!" I holler at Lilibeth.

Bitch has no right to touch my kid, but with superhuman strength she's got Sebastian out of the stroller. She's holding him close to her chest. He'd been strapped in—at least I think I strapped him in—so I'm shocked that she's swooped him up so damn quickly. He's heavy, but she seems not to feel the weight.

"He's bleeding," she says. "His dear face."

I grab him from her, and she releases. I see his eyeball *is* bleeding. And he's holding his right hand in his left. Tears spill from both the bloodied eye and the clear one. The two rivers, blood and salt, meet on his sweet-baby-boy cheek and grow pink.

"What happened, sweet pea?" I ask, my heart pounding with already knowing that this is Lucia's doing.

I make him open his hurt eye enough to see that it's still there.

A bit red but intact. Next, I peel his hurt hand away from his other and see there is a full set of teeth marks just below his thumb. So many teeth, more than seem credible.

Lucia has the habit of gnawing on her brother. My husband thought it was adorable when she'd suck on her brother's thumb or his little toes instead of her own. Now, she isn't just sucking his thumb, she looks as if she's ready to tear it away from the rest of his hand with her creepy teeth. Gnaw on its base until the whole thing comes loose.

Lucia was born with teeth; although that's a thing I now know happens—rare but still possible—it still and will forever gross me out. Her toothy, newborn baby grin added to the devilish look in her eyes. And that devilish look doesn't even go away when she sleeps, because she sleeps with her eyes open. Not all the way but enough so that there is a white sliver at the bottom of each eye. Sometimes her pupils interrupt the slight moon of white, and it's like she's watching us even in her sleep, like she's one of those paintings where the eyes seem to follow you.

She will be thirteen weeks soon, and somehow in the last few days, she's grown even faster than before. Like, all the teeth an adult is supposed to have are coming in, all except perhaps the wisdom teeth. They burst through her gums like they were joining the damn parade. Her sinkhole of a mouth flipped inside out, and nothing became something, a Grand Canyon of peaks and valleys—her great hunk of a tongue a river amid it all.

"She bit him," Lilibeth says.

"I'm well fucking aware," I say. I've been having more and more trouble keeping my nasty monologue internal these days. The other day my husband blinked at me twice after I'd said something or other, then he simply said, "You're getting kinda mean." It was the factual way he said it that pissed me off.

"I need to stop cursing," I say, which isn't really an apology, is it?

"She was also poking him. In the eye."

"What?"

I turn my attention to Lucia, who, I swear to God, is staring up at the sky like an old man who just took a sneaky bite of the Thanksgiving pie. Practically twiddling her thumbs and whistling.

I lean in close. Get her to put her eyes on mine.

"What did you do?" I ask in an adult voice and not the sweet, lilting voice I use for the other kids.

My body is blocking Lilibeth's view of Lucia, so she doesn't see my little girl sit up straight with the strength of a twenty-year-old Pilates instructor and speak her first words to me or to anyone.

"I eat," she says with a smile so wide I can see her creepy molars in her creepy baby mouth.

This child. This little Lucia Lucifer is just three months, and she is so full of teeth and words that I feel sick.

"Did you hear that?" I ask Lilibeth as I straighten up.

Lilibeth isn't listening to me or to Lucia. She's staring at

Sebastian, making soothing sounds and stroking my son's head. She's squatting down so low I know she is going to need help standing back up. She is making him laugh now. Wiping his face with a white cotton handkerchief that she carries in her pocket like this was some other century.

"He's okay," Lilibeth says, and holds her hands up to me—palms down, knuckles up—for help rising.

I look down at her, and I see that she is a child too or becoming one again. We grow needier and needier by the day. We are born. We are uncomfortable. We wither.

I reach out and help Lilibeth stand. Her loneliness, her endless conversations. They are no different than what I get from Sebastian or Jeremy when I come home from an outing. They love the attention. Want to be held. I hear her knees creak as she stands, but it doesn't seem to faze her. She glances at Lucia, and I see that look I catch on people's faces right before they say, "She looks like you." A little realization. A little horror. Only this time it doesn't disappear quite as fast.

She looks at me and whispers, "It looked like she was trying to scoop out his eyeball with her pointer finger."

"Don't be crazy," I say, stunning myself with this response. This is the second time someone has given me the opportunity to speak of my worry about Lucia. And what did I do with this opportunity? I ignored it. Shat on it.

Sure, I've asked my husband questions like, "Does she seem right to you?" Or "Do you feel like she's different than the others?" And "Don't you think her fingernails look like talons?" All questions he never answers. He just laughs with that dismissiveness he offers when he thinks I'm being a silly girl. And now, on the street, I do it to Lilibeth.

"Maybe I saw it wrong," she says.

"Maybe you did," I snap back, surprising myself yet again.

Lilibeth winces.

"You okay, sweetie?" I say to my son.

"I okay," he says.

"See, he's fine." My tone is nasty.

"You know . . ." Lilibeth starts.

"What?"

"It isn't always the mother's fault."

"What isn't?" I snap.

"Bad seed behavior."

"Are you saying there is something wrong with my kid?" My heart pounds faster. She's seen! She knows! For a moment my heart swells with love for Lilibeth: Can a kindred spirit exist after all?

"No. Of course not," she says, daring to look genuinely horrified. "She's a sweet baby angel." Lilibeth pauses and considers her next step with me as if she is walking on glass, then says, "You know, I'm not practicing anymore, but I do still have many colleagues in the field who are and some of them specialize in family issues, if you want me to connect you."

"Jesus Christ."

Lilibeth has the nerve to reach out and touch my arm. I shake her off.

"I'm saying motherhood isn't easy. You don't always like your children. You love them, but you don't *like* them. I don't like my eldest much these days—I only have the two. He's selfish. Cares about money more than his own family. They tell us we aren't supposed to have favorites, but we do. And I think that's okay. Your favorite kid is the one giving you the least trouble. That's all there is to it, don't you think?"

"Why don't you fuck right off," I say and see her step back as if I'm going to hit her.

I yank Sebastian off his feet and shove him back into the stroller. I buckle him in and right myself.

"I didn't mean . . ." Lilibeth is stammering, and I almost feel bad about how I've treated her. Almost.

"Roadrunner!" Sebastian exclaims and points ahead. Lilibeth and I look.

Flightless birds have always struck me as useless. Penguins are absurd. Chickens are beyond stupid—thank you, Alex Forrest, for proving that to be correct—but at least you can eat them. What's the point of an inedible bird that can't even fly? My mother, however, loves roadrunners—she likes anything with hidden murderous instincts.

Lilibeth, on the other hand, bends at the waist and locks eyes with my son. She makes it perfectly clear that she is speaking only to him.

"They are actually called greater roadrunners, and they are from the cuckoo family. They can run up to fifteen miles an hour, and they are omnivorous. That means they eat all kinds of things—insects, prickly pears, seeds, and lizards. Even small rattlesnakes!"

"That little idiot better be careful," I offer, the meanness oozing out of me like venom. "Coyotes love to eat roadrunners, just like in the cartoons."

"How fast the coyotes?" he says. He is articulate for his age, my son, but he skips words in his sentences as if he's hoarding them for his future mansplaining.

"Oh, very fast. Thirty-five or forty miles per hour," I say. I sound bored, but my heart is racing. Before Lucia, my past was a pileup of dead things that I could step over if I was careful enough—tied closed with the properly sized bandana. Then came Lucia. Lucia with her monstrousness and unavoidability. She's the speed bump I can't ignore. The house I birthed—a monster inside a monster inside a monster.

"Yes, well," Lilibeth says and gives Sebastian's cheek another wipe with the handkerchief before handing it back to me. I take it. "I always picture myself a roadrunner. Fast and smart and ready to survive in the roughest of circumstances."

"They're actually quite brutal," I say, trying to think of what I can add to make Lilibeth feel stupid.

"Yes, well," she says, as I sputter out and meander away from whatever insult I was scraping for.

"Ki-oat," Lucia says. She points to her own chest with her chubby baby fingers.

"She's a predator," Lilibeth says in wonderment.

"Only aspirationally," I say, and it's a joke. I'm clearly making a joke, but there is a tremor in my voice. One made by fear. Fear of Lucia. Fear that Lucia's freakishness has finally been found out. Fear that I can't raise a female creature who is obviously already so much stronger and smarter than I am.

Fear, most of all, that Lilibeth now knows Lucia is on her way to becoming an unstoppable beast.

I look at Lilibeth, and she looks at me. Lilibeth is pale, her shoulders hunched forward as if her whole body is ready to curl up into a ball if need be. She blinks once, twice, then, for one moment, Lilibeth and I are fully connected. Fear bounces between us, and I almost tell her everything. Spill my guts about all the weird shit Lucia has done since the day she was born. I almost tell her that I'm worried Lucia is stronger, smarter, more volatile than either of her parents. Than anyone we've ever met. I almost tell Lilibeth that I'm not up to the task of raising Lucia. On the tip of my tongue sit questions I am not comfortable with: *What if we are not safe? What if I've made a monster who can't be tamed?* And finally, *What kind of mother calls her daughter a monster?*

I watch Lilibeth's face struggle with her own questions before settling back into a troubled and willful silence.

I fill in the blanks for her with the phrase everyone always says when they are, at first, troubled by Lucia. "I know, I know. She looks just like me." I hear it differently now that I'm the one saying it. As if what's being said is how much one monstrous creature resembles the other. "Shit," I mumble.

"Shit, shit, shit," Sebastian says, and old lady Lilibeth laughs.

The tension breaks. Sweet Sebastian has a way of easing everything.

"I was always glad I didn't have daughters," Lilibeth says and sees my surprise. She waves it away with her right hand. "I know, I know. It makes me a terrible feminist, but I was so scared of watching someone go through what I went through as a girl. And nothing all that terrible happened to me, but puberty for girls is rough. It just is, and I knew I'd try to save her from that, and the saving would look something like taming. And aren't the boys the ones that deserve some taming? Haven't girls been subduing themselves for long enough?"

"I suppose," I say, my voice grumpy, a mask to hide my quaking vulnerability.

"What if you just let her be the coyote?" Lilibeth asks.

"What does that mean?"

Lilibeth laughs again, at herself this time, before adding, "Oh, heck, I don't know, but what if we women weren't so afraid of ourselves. Of each other? Then what?"

It's a hopeful thought, but also improbable. Plus, it's Sebastian Lilibeth pats on the head in goodbye, not Lucia. Her own advice still too scary to follow.

I push the stroller forward and put in my AirPods without saying goodbye.

"Me out," Sebastian says over and over, so I don't get far before I'm stopping again to help him out of his seat. This walk is already doomed. No exercise for me, so might as well let him look at each and every rock along the roadside.

I make sure Lucia is still strapped in and pull the restraint a little tighter.

"Mama," she says, and I swear to God she winks at me.

v v

Dillon has gone to work this afternoon, and the kids and I are inside trying to stay cool. I do not sing. Not to any of my kids. I do not even sing "Happy Birthday," but I do list things. Long lists in a soft voice will put them to sleep just as much as anything else. Lists of chores I must do. Lists of things I hate. Lists of places I've been or want to go. Grocery lists in the right tone can work. Sebastian and Jeremy are already napping. Lucia, as per usual, refuses, so we sit in the thick-walled house my husband built for a family he didn't know at the time, and I recite my list of female villains, humming to fill the spaces when my memory stumbles.

"Harley Quinn," I say. "Poison Ivy, Medusa, Nurse Ratched!"

Lucia listens with endearing attention. Her too-blue eyes look at my mouth, studying the sounds.

I'm tired and tomorrow we need to finally remember to drive our trash to the transfer station. The bear-safe cans we keep just outside are full, and while they keep the bears out, they don't do a great job sealing in the stink. I can smell the waste of the past few weeks finding its way inside the house. It's the sour smell of sunbaked remnants, and it always reminds me of the dumpster outside that first apartment I remember living in with my mom. The metal would heat up too hot to touch, the insides baked soupy within a week. A whole complex of discarded materials and the smell of it would sneak in under our front door. Sometimes the smell was so bad it would wake me and my mom in the middle of the night.

In the late eighties, we lived in a one-bedroom apartment in what was and still is considered a bad part of Albuquerque, which is kind of hilarious since Albuquerque is made up of bad parts. The area where we lived was and is still called the War Zone, and I remember the war of it well. There were bars over our windows on which birds would sit, painting the black bars white with their droppings and bringing mites into the small, dark apartment. Little yellow things that the landlord called chicken bugs—I assume for their yellow, plucked color. They got into our clothes and rug and cloth shower curtain. Turns out their official name *is* chicken mites, and they aren't yellow in color at all, but white, turning a reddish hue once fed. I must have changed the color in my mind due to the name, but even now, I picture them a pimpled-up yellow. Little piss eaters.

Regardless of color or visibility, they were nasty, and so were those birds. Rat birds—pigeons and sparrows. Garbage birds who shat buckets and shook their parasites into our little cave of a world and deserved to be sprayed with racoon piss.

I didn't watch *A Nightmare on Elm Street* until I was a teenager. Long after I moved out of that apartment, but some years later, as soon as I saw Nancy's mother, Marge, put those bars on Nancy's bedroom window, I felt a kinship to Nancy that perhaps the movie did not intend. In the film, Marge, an alcoholic, not entirely unlike my mother—although my mother applied her addiction to self-involvement and secrets more than liquor—believes the barred-up window and the locked bedroom door will protect Nancy from Freddy Krueger. An absurd effort since Freddy gets in through your mind. Still, crazy begets crazy, and just like with me and my mom, there was and is always the craving for security even when you know the monster is already in the house.

I've craved every brand of safety, even when it's false. Hell, I got fucking married because I thought it would make me feel safe. In the end, we're all gonna get slashed cunt to throat by some burnt guy's nail extensions. That burnt guy buried himself inside us long ago, but he isn't even the real threat. The real threat is Marge. Marge who opened the door to evil even as she pretended to lock it out.

Anyway, while the birds were nasty and the apartment dark, I felt safe in it for a time. Safer than I should have, I suppose. I believed my mother when she told me my father didn't love us enough to stay. That her family didn't care to know her. Or me. I believed the simplicity of her answers. I believed that the past could be erased. I believed this for a long time.

The War Zone during the day seemed more like the aftermath of some seismic event we'd barely missed. The dead still on the field but not doing anyone any harm. It didn't scare me. Who could care at that point?

What I remember most about living in the War Zone was watching television on the little black-and-white TV my mother bought us at Village Thrift. It had silver antennae that could be manipulated to pick up at least three channels. It had surprisingly good volume that I loved to turn all the way up, my nose almost touching the fuzz of the screen. The sound hid noises that came from my mother's bedroom when she had visitors (and to be fair, she only ever had one visitor at a time and a tendency to be chronically monogamous even when the horror of said single boyfriend became quite clear). The stories the screen sizzled into the room helped me focus, so I could ignore the bold nudity of her boyfriend as he crossed from bedroom to bathroom. For the most part, he ignored me too. I didn't exist. And it meant she'd forget to tie my jaw shut; my foot brace stayed tucked under the bed. It was a deal kept sacred by almost all parties.

On that TV, I watched cartoons—Scooby-Doo and the Smurfs and the one where they all had snorkels for noses. I watched Mister Rogers even though I thought it was too young for me. In the evening, sometimes, my mom would join me for *The Muppet Show*. I watched everything as hard as I could, nose to screen, memorizing character names and lines, as if I might be required to repeat them someday.

My favorite thing of all things were the *Wonder Woman* re-runs. Lynda Carter with her tiny waist and her gold bracelets. Three seasons and fifty-nine episodes. In the very first episode of Season 1—not that I saw them in order, but still—they introduce Baroness von Gunther. I loved that character. In my defense, it was only much, much later that I realized the baroness was a Nazi and that Nazis were far from a thing to be envied or emu-lated. Anyway, I was a kid. I saw a pretty blonde with plans and thought: *That's the one. I'm gonna be her.* I saw that women could be conniving and gorgeous and a bit in love with each other all at once.

I moved on to bigger and better villains pretty quickly. Once I realized a woman could be the source of the wrong, the evil, the world tilted in a way that made much more sense. I looked for her everywhere. Craved her. Made lists of her. Shows and movies always. *God, I want that*, I thought. Give me a bat and pigtails and call me powerful. Maleficent! At first, little kid me thought the same thing Sleeping Beauty's parents thought: *Who'd want that old bitch at the party?!* But then I read and dug and realized how gorgeous she was. How sad and separate. She hadn't left her home in decades. She was an angry old fairy, because the world had forgotten her, left her to sit with her nose pressed to a screen while they birthed and rallied. Then they sharpened Angelina Jolie's cheekbones and built her some wild horns, and I knew I'd been right. I knew they were all me.

I wanted my origin story—like Catwoman, who fell out the window breathing her last breath as she was nibbled to death by felines. Dr. Harleen Quinzel dumped in a vat of chemicals only to be blanched white and dredged up insane. I obsessed on how to get my mother to tell it to me, to trick her into saying more, but she never caved. Did she have an origin story? Was she the villain too? I begged. I cried. I left lists of villains I knew about the apartment and asked her to check the box next to the one I was most like. She never played. Never even gave me a wink to let me know I was close. I didn't know what questions to ask. The order in which to put the words to get the right answer. I suppose I was living my origin story. There I was in a barred house, locked inside with Marge the monster and whatever Krueger she chose to let in that month.

I remember the cool of my mother's apartment but also how the bedroom would heat up at night because we could not or would not open the windows. My mother's body in the middle of the bed, barely a buffer between her and her boyfriend.

I would move to the living room when I could, my feet forgetfully untethered from the persistent brace. I would lie on the floor in front of my beloved television, as close as I could get to the screen and still see, so that I could keep the volume low. Still, my mother would find me in the night.

"Why are you out here again?" she asked as she gathered me up.

"Mama, nooo," I said and clawed for the screen, cat scratching her arms.

"Stop that! Right now!" She dropped me on the floor, but it didn't hurt. "I'm bleeding!" she shouted and shoved her arms into my face. The red streaks looked like ribbons.

"What's wrong out there?" he said from the bedroom.

"Shhhh," I said. Panicked.

"Get up right now and come to bed," she said. "Don't make me tie your arms down too."

I did as I was told.

How things looked to other people was important to my mother. When we were outside of the house, she loved me openly. Held my hand. Laughed. Took me with her to events to show me off. I was pretty. I was smart. I was mature. People marveled at how young she was and how good she was. At home, the act was less thorough. Knots were tied tighter in private. Her temper was louder. Her absence stronger. But, when she had a new man, the act came into the house. She was a good mommy. Her daughter was adored.

"We tell each other everything," she said.

"I learn from watching her grow," she'd offer.

"I can't imagine my life without my daughter. She practically raises herself!"

"I love you, Mommy," I'd say back. My limbs unencumbered. The television at my disposal. And I did love her. I did.

The problem, as you get older, is that you realize the world feels a responsibility to hate. So, I forgot my mother for a long time. Forgot that I was faking. I left the villains behind and had Jeremy and Sebastian instead. I promised myself I'd be so much better at mothering than she had ever been. My children would be free. They'd know love and be allowed to roar as loud as they wanted in the high desert.

˅ ˅

The walls on a hay bale house like this one keep the cool air in and the hot air out. The windows are set back so there is a good foot of ledge before the glass panes that swing out. My husband built it with great care and forethought—the concrete floor smoothed and stained into iron swirls. So, I sit on the cool floor with Lucia; the unforgiving surface hurts my tailbone, makes my hips ache, but I do it anyway. The discomfort surely something I am owed.

"More bad guys. Say more," Lucia says, drool dripping down her chin. Too many teeth and too big a tongue, I suppose. Lucia drools like a little goblin and yet the skin on her face is soft and pink and perfect.

"That's right," I say. "Bad guys. Or maybe gals."

"More," she says.

I offer more, noting not for the first time that the fictional ones especially don't have a lot of grit to them. If I were going to write a good female villain, she would best all the men. Her kind of evil would be thorough and lasting. She would not get caught. She would not care. She'd be Patrick Bateman with a vagina and tits. And a dead uterus, so no sneaky man juice could get up there to make its own spot of baby. Not some wicked witch melting away when splashed with water. Fuck that.

"Most people aren't truly good or truly evil. The wicked are rare." I hear myself say this with longing. A wistfulness for the wicked.

"Wicked," she says, and not in the way a Bostonian would say, as in "wicked cool," but in the way a villainess would.

I want to be proud, but Lucia's beauty, her fat neck combined with her absurdly advanced language, gives me chills. I don't understand her, and a mother should understand her child.

"The baroness was my favorite. A spy. Wonder Woman was singular minded, but the baroness, she was always shifting, planning, making. All you had to do to defeat Wonder Woman was have any dumb man chain her bracelets together. The baroness, on the other hand, changed her whole being to survive!"

I look at Lucia. Really look. And I feel small, like I am still that little girl on the apartment floor looking up at the sky of my mother. But I must be more than that little girl ever imagined she'd have to be. I must be more than I have been for Sebastian and Jeremy.

"They were in love. Wonder Woman and the baroness," I say to Lucia. She accepts the statement and tucks it into the fat little folds of her neck for safekeeping as if it hasn't come out of nowhere. "Of course, a man wrote those comics, and all men can imagine is women fondling each other. But still. It was something."

Lucia giggles as if she understands. The front of her onesie is soaked through with her drool.

"Now, Bellatrix Lestrange, she was created by a woman. A villain almost as evil as the main one, although I don't know why she couldn't have been central to it all. Even women can't or won't imagine the full potential of other women. Still, she had those hollow eyes. That laugh. She did not give two fucks. Love her."

"Love her," Lucia purrs, and the unnatural words, the tiny fat face, the fingers that squeeze at air as if it is substance make me feel uneasy, sick to my stomach.

"Gross," I say. Even I don't know what I mean.

"Groshhhh, grosh, grosh," she says.

"I don't like that," I say, still not knowing specifically what I mean. I don't like being repeated. True. I don't like how she slurs her "s" into a "shhhh" while spit flings from her freakishly large teeth. True. I don't like how much of Lucia looks to be like so much of me. True. True. True.

She does not repeat this last phrase but rather goes back to drooling and stacking little colored blocks in a half-focused way that suggests boredom. She is smart, this one. Too smart, and that brings the sick in my stomach to a new pain, a cramping of muscles that makes me stand quickly, stretch tall to stop the inward curling. She looks up at me, the sudden tall, tall tree of her mother, and I see not her, not me, but my mother. She'd say, "I need my bestie." She'd swoop me up and into the dark, dark hot we'd go. "You can't leave me alone with *him*," she'd say, and I'd get as close to her neck as I could. It was where her smell was the best.

She would take long baths, my mother. I would beg her to keep the water in the tub for me when she got out. The soapy white of that water still warm. She'd say no. I'd ask again. "No way," she'd say. Again, I'd ask. "I just shaved my legs in there!" she'd declare, but the fourth time, she'd say yes, and I'd slip into that soapy, dirty Mom water and feel so, so safe.

⌄ ⌄

Sitting on the floor with one's kids, watching them play mindless games, leaves lots of time for the mind to wander. I stare out the window at our shed. Its one window stares back at me, and I remember that my mother unloaded a bunch of boxes on us, downsizing, she said, right at the time I was about to have Lucia. We tucked those boxes away in our shed. There was no time for me to even wonder about what might be inside, but Lucia is making me want to remember what I looked like as a child. Were there pictures of me? Pictures my mother hadn't curated for the picture frames on her walls. I think there was a box marked "Thea's photos and things."

I used to take photographs with a Polaroid camera that I lost long ago in some move or another. I loved that camera, and I would have taken hundreds if the film hadn't been expensive. Still, I remember now that I took a lot. I head out to the shed to find this box of photos, thinking perhaps a truer version of my childhood might be quilted together somewhere inside of them.

We have no attic, no basement, but we have an outbuilding, a kind of starter shed that Dillon built to teach himself how to build a full house. It's where we keep stuff that we don't want but feel we shouldn't throw out—lately, it's full of arts and crafts from the kids, but it's also stocked with my mother's off-loaded boxes.

The sun is high and hot. "A dry heat," people say—as if that is some kind of fucking victory. Dry or wet, it is the kind of heat you know will kill you, wants to kill you, and you are a fool for thinking you can live in it, settle it as if you are a cowboy and it is a wild horse.

I wish I had my sunglasses, but only for a second. Soon I'm opening the old door that Dillon repurposed for the shed and stepping into the cool dark. I shut the door behind me and breathe. I smell heat gone stale. I smell old papers going crisp with desert. We don't have scorpions here, but we do have spiders and rattlesnakes. Rattlesnakes like the sun—hot rocks and the center of red dirt trails. Spiders like the dark. We've found more than one brown recluse out here. It's a necrotic spider, so if bitten, your skin will blister and rot. The females are the most danger-ous. They have more prominent glands, bigger bodies, and lon-ger fangs. Peter Parker would rot and die if bitten by a female of the species long before Spider-Man could even imagine his own existence.

I stomp my Crocced feet to let them know I've arrived. It's what you are supposed to do if you see a mountain lion or a bear. Don't run. Make yourself big and make some noise. I tell myself it works with spiders too. My eyes adjust to the dark, and I find the shelves that keep our boxes off the ground. Grab the one I know is marked "Thea/Photo." As much as I'd love the privacy of the small space, I make my way back out into the sun, then to the kitchen table. I leave the necrotic venom behind.

"What're you doing, sweetie?" my husband is wearing cargo shorts and a T-shirt so old it has lost its hem.

I point to the box.

"Cool, can I look with you?"

Fuck. His breath smells of beef jerky. Mountain folks love jerky, like it's a fucking delicacy. Pop-up beef jerky stands rise out of the desert as if they are a specialty item and not just plastic-wrapped, repurposed roadkill. My husband falls for it every time. Buys bags of them and chats up the men selling the shit like he's looking for a new best friend. Is he looking for a new best friend? I thought I was his best friend. I guess I'm failing at that too.

"Sure," I say.

I pull out old photos. The Polaroid years show a healthy baby. Smiles. Head tilted in thought. Not fat or dumb. I can see the smart in my own baby eyes. There are few from older years. The Polaroids die out, then there are only the pictures from disposable cameras, some of them developed special so they'd have the date stamped in the corner. I am tall and lovely. Shy or pretending to be. My skin clear. I feel sorry for the girl in the pictures. She is me and not me. She looks unsure. I find a picture of my mother next, with her boyfriend. The one who stayed with us in the War Zone. He is tall and handsome. A sick feeling blooms in my chest. What was his name? Daryl? David? Does it matter? The feeling of dread that comes from just seeing his face makes me nauseated. I drop myself into a chair. The photos flop in my hands.

I can't find any of the photos I took. Not a one. My mother did not think there was any other way to see me besides the way she wanted me to be seen, and she certainly didn't think there was value in studying how I saw the world. The realization of it shouldn't even be a realization to me at this point, but I feel its devastation all the same.

"What if all our memories are really just the stories we've been told over the years?" I ask Dillon.

"Huh?" he says.

"Like, what if it isn't how it happened at all, or what we think we looked like isn't what we actually looked like. For example, what if I remember my old rope swing wrong? I remember it as special, because my mother told me it was and because in the photo *she* took, I am happy. But really, the rope swing was dirty and unstable and terrifying."

"What rope swing?"

"The swing doesn't fucking matter. I'm asking what if what I know about myself isn't true. Doesn't your parent shape your story for you?"

"What difference does it make?"

"It's a lot of power, isn't it? Think of the influence we have over our kids. We're already shaping their story. We must be!"

Somehow my husband has found a bowl of cereal and is eating it next to me, the milk dripping out his mouth, onto his spoon, and back into the bowl.

"It's a bit overwhelming if you say it like that," he says, but I can't stop.

I am outraged, yet curious. "My mother told me what I was, so I was. Does it matter that I wasn't? If, for example, I think Lucia is a monster, does that make her a monster? Will it make her into a monster? Maybe what I see in her is me, and I'm the monster, or maybe I was never the monster. Maybe my mother just told me I was the monster. Or told me I couldn't be the monster!" My voice rises as my thoughts babble out of me and Dillon's eyes widen. His chewing stops.

"You think our daughter is a monster?" he asks, sounding sad.

"Listen," I say, unwilling to stop my thought process or even quiet it. "What if things happened that I can't or won't remember? Or that I remember, but thought were my fault. I was five years old, and somehow, I thought I was old enough to handle things that no one is old enough to handle. What if I'm fucking up Lucia in the same way? Telling her she's some kind of freak when she just needs me to see her? Really see her. Do you know what I mean?"

"Are you okay?" he asks. He does not know what I mean. "You seem a little manic."

"Don't you mean hysterical?" I spit at him.

"Hey, now, I didn't say that."

I'm about to tell him to fuck right off when Lucia walks out of the bedroom. She doesn't scooch or crawl. She walks. She is thirteen weeks and walking. Upstaging me in the midst of my tantrum.

"Holy shit," he says and drops his bowl onto the table. Milk splashes on my mother's photos. They will be forever sticky, gritty with cereal. I feel an overwhelming sadness. It is huge and dark. Cold as the storage shed. The corners of it just as poisonous. "She's walking!"

She is. Walking. Arms out like a mummy.

Lucia moves to her daddy and into his joy. He is distracted.

Totally removed from the moment I was trying to have with him. From me.

"PAY ATTENTION TO ME!" I scream at him. "I WAS TALKING TO YOU!" Lucia looks at me with glee, my husband with horror.

I am *in hysterics*, I think. *This is me hysterical.*

I think, *My mother was a terrible mother, so now I am a terrible mother.*

I go to our bedroom and slam the door behind me. I push books off the nightstand and flip our mattress. I pick up a pillow and scream into it until my voice refuses to make more sound.

˅ ˅

Hours later, I emerge. I am all cried out. The rage put back to bed.

"Falafel and rice?" I say to Dillon with my croak of a voice. He looks scared of me, but I don't care.

"Sure," he says. He's been watching his phone while I melted down. He answers me without looking up from it.

"We don't have a green," I say. "Do you want to run out to the garden and get one?"

"Are you okay?" he asks, actually looking at me.

"Fine," I say, clearly not.

"I put Lucia down for her nap. She wore herself out," he says.

No shit, I think.

"Kale?" he asks. His voice already growing choppy with a return to inattention. He's always looking at his stupid phone.

"What are you watching now?" I say, my voice a whisper.

"This crazy chick," he says. He holds out his device so I can see yet another middle-aged white woman losing her shit in public for the entertainment of the entire World Wide Web. Somehow, he doesn't connect that my bedroom tantrum doesn't look all that different from the woman's on the screen. *Idiot.*

It has puzzled me that anyone is surprised by these displays of recorded rage. Sure, the vitriol might be ugly or misplaced, but it doesn't surprise me. Female rage is hardly a rarity. We are all about to burst—a simmering pot of violence that the world has yet to know. Why would anyone be surprised that we've reached our midpoint in life and are finally willing to lose our shit for the rest of recorded history?

Where is the rage supposed to go?

I shove Dillon's phone away.

Fuck off, I think. "Kale," I say. "Tomatoes too."

He sighs, disappointed that I do not appreciate the suffering in the same way he does. And there he is. A giver-upper. His curiosity about our menace of a daughter, his raging wife, and this internet bitch dried up just like that. Simple man.

"Go," I say. He sighs and puts his phone down. It slides into the couch cushion, so I know when he comes back inside, he won't know where it is. There will be a lengthy skit where he searches for it, too scared to ask me if I know. It makes me mad, knowing what I know is coming.

Guilt makes me pinch my nose, clench my eyes shut. He's a good man, my husband. Kind and sweet and hardworking. He loves his children. He loves me. He is naïve. He is not afraid of what is coming. And what is coming? When I look at my youngest daughter, I almost know.

The back door slams behind him, waking Jeremy from his nap. *It's all right, though*, I tell myself. *He should have already been up.* It's almost dinner, so this late of a nap means bedtime will not be easy. A good mom would keep a better schedule.

"Where's Daddy?" Jeremy asks, rubbing at his sleepy eyes, and I point.

"Go help him harvest, please," I say. "Take your brother."

The eldest does what he's told, and I hear him telling his little brother to put on his "crocodiles" so that they can "be helpful." My heart swells with love. Was I ever that good? Probably not. I see very little of myself in Jeremy. And, of course, why would I? His childhood has been blessed. He has a dad. A home. Even if I totally shit the bed, my kids will be fine. All except Lucia, of course.

To my detriment, I had only my mother, and I only had her when she needed me to show the world how good she was. I learned the rotting feeling of loneliness young and I called it love. I'm still waiting to make that mistake, whatever it will be. My eldest feels none of that. He feels safe. He feels loved. He has a bed that soaks him in so many stuffed animals that I worry he will suffocate. My second son too. He knows no fear. He runs and jumps and smiles and laughs. He has tears for a scraped knee or a desire not met, but he knows nothing harsh. The world is right for him. Lucia. She is different. She is a girl with a mother who is unsure what she is made of. A mother who raised herself but did so too early and without a guide.

˅ ˅

Dillon has been out in the garden far longer than necessary. At least now he can watch his kids at the same time—a little multitasking he would never opt for on his own. Like all things a husband does, he gathers food far too slowly, as if somehow life is still about cherishing the small moments. The fuck it is. There are bathrooms to be cleaned. Shit to be wiped off toilet bowls, washed off clothes, and, somehow, walls. Groceries to be bought. Thank-you cards to be written. Naps to be forced. And yet, he takes his time. I watch him out there, enjoying the sun. I tell him sometimes, "I envy your life." He thinks I'm being funny.

I do try to give him credit where credit is due. The mountains of New Mexico are not the friendliest place to grow vegetables, but Dillon has made it happen in spades. He does not take no for an answer. What man does? Instead, he picks up truckloads of fresh manure at the transit station and snakes hosing that he has pinpricked with a nail in a painstaking manner—again, acting as if we have all the time in the world. He's managed to cultivate something with a bit of substance out of the dust and clay we call earth. We eat from it daily when the season allows, and it is impressive.

The spring this year was especially dry. No rain. Only heat. Fires in the Pecos and down in Carnuel, where the flames leapt the highway, burning tiny little homes that were already having a hard time surviving. They had to close 66 and the highway, and Dillon got stuck at the office. Had to rent himself a hotel room in the city so he could get some good sleep. Meanwhile, I was here with three children, one of whom certainly had pink eye or butt worm or hoof-and-mouth disease or some such nasty. Anyhow, that was when the first cucumbers were up—early since he grew them indoors for a bit—and he was luxuriating in some hotel while I was harvesting cucumbers for a salad only to discover they were bitter and spiky.

While the cucumbers grew in abundance, obscene in their length and girth, they had this poisonous flavor. I researched it for my husband, seeing how sad he was that no one would eat his spiky, bitter cucumber—he didn't even believe me when I told him. He said, "I'll see about it when I get home." As if he could change the taste by simply taking a look-see. Since then, we have learned that the prickly outsides and bitter taste develop in viny fruit when they feel threatened by their environment.

I wonder if this is also true of Lucia. While it's true that I was happier during her pregnancy than any other, perhaps she sensed my giving in, my giving up. My bitterness so deep that I couldn't even taste it anymore, but she could. The environment she was born into was hostile, so she's making herself bitter, all her little hair follicles gaining a poke like those cucumber skins, so no one would ever dare take a bite.

Or maybe it's simpler than all that. Maybe the women in this family are evil.

I can hear Lucia in her crib, banging on the bar with her palms. She doesn't cry or holler. She demands. No question in her mind that if she rings the bell I will come running. And I do. I walk swiftly to her door and open it, resolved to protect her and guide her through this ugly, ugly world that hates the *idea* of her, let alone her real and growing body.

But the Lucia I find in her crib doesn't seem bitter or prickly. She is just Lucia. She is happy. Deadly set, in fact, in her happiness. Did I mention that she loves those damn cucumbers? Loves them. She doesn't think they taste nasty. She likes them washed but not peeled. She sucks on them. Leaves her cruel little bite marks up and down their exterior.

"Mama," she says in an entirely too adult voice.

"Yes, baby," I say.

It's then that I notice the crib is missing a chunk. The top wooden bar where each of my children has clung with their small hands as they waited for me to come in and rescue them from their solitude is cut in half. Correction. Bitten in half.

Lucia looks up at me with a wide, bright smile on her face. Her hands hold the two halves of the bar—she's gnawed them.

I follow one leg of the dark wood with my eyes and see that the bite marks run its length. All the way from my daughter's hand to the crib corner. Her teeth have sunk into the wood over and over again.

"You building a lodge?" I ask, wondering where my calm comes from.

How long has she been doing this? Surely, I would have noticed before this moment. I look at the other rails. Her marks are everywhere.

My girl's bite marks are deep. They dig into the meat of the wood—the soft, lighter parts—and they are layered. Like she's bitten in each place once, then again. An outer bite and an inner bite.

She sits her bottom back down on the mattress while I inspect the crib. It's covered with her marks. Every damn inch. Was she just in here chewing away this whole time? I was having a tantrum, and she was feasting. The crib is ruined. There will be no saving it, and I feel a wash of sadness. I bought this for Jeremy. It's not an heirloom or anything, but I thought maybe we could make it one. That I'd pass it on to Jeremy when he had kids. It was not cheap, after all. Simply structured, but made from black walnut.

Life is just a slow wearing away of the soul. This is what I'm thinking when Lucia opens her mouth and points inside.

"What?" I ask. She points again. Insistent. "Something in there? A splinter?" Perhaps she's cut. Perhaps she's choking on a whole chunk of wood.

I lean in. Farther. I look into the open slit of her mouth. There are her teeth—a full row of them but somehow bigger. Baby teeth usually have a kind of wavy edge to them, a bumpy surface that makes them look temporary. I love this soft little nudge of an age. Lucia's teeth, however, are bigger, more solid, their top edge flat as the safe side of a knife blade. She opens her mouth wider, puts her finger inside. I lean closer, my stomach resting on the splintery edge of the split crib.

Inside her otherwise tiny mouth are two rows of teeth. The front set is new. I can see how they've pushed up in front of her baby teeth, eclipsing them in height. She still has all her baby teeth—I count twenty, which is a number Jeremy didn't have until he was three and Sebastian still doesn't have—and somehow these twenty are behind thirty-two adult teeth that weren't there this morning.

"Jesus fuck," I say into my daughter's mouth.

I'm looking into the mouth of a great white whose teeth have been filed down for safety purposes, only this feels far from safe. The teeth are packed in front to back in ways that don't seem possible, and as I look, trying to comprehend the extent of all that bony white, her mouth widens. It widens more. I get closer. Her breath smells milky like a baby's should, but also woody, a result of swallowing the whole forest of her crib, I suppose. And at the back of her throat, there's her double uvula—split into two, it hangs huge in her throat like a barely parted curtain.

I knew about the split uvula before this moment. The doctor pointed it out in the hospital. They told me it was fine. To consider it a spot of luck. "Imagine she's got a wishbone back there!" he'd exclaimed.

I already knew he was wrong. So, I didn't really listen. It was only later at home when I thought about that image. My mom used to dry the wishbones out on the windowsill for weeks. Some years, forgetting it was there until it was brittle and bleached. Alone, always alone, I would give it a pull, yank one side from the other, always winning both the smaller and the larger piece. Wish granted. And how sick is that metaphor for a doctor to hand a mother? As if Lucia could be opened and split in half. Who would pull? Me on one end and my mother on the other? Would I win?

Lucia giggles and starts to spit out her teeth, one at a time. Just her baby teeth, I realize. They clack on the ground, gather at my feet. She wipes spit off her chin when she is done, and the teeth that are left inside her mouth gain harsher edges, points even.

She is still chubby. Her cheeks full. Her belly round. The chunks of her legs barely give way to her knees. Still, she stands like an adult and holds out her arms to me.

"Come," she says.

I rush to her. Because I am afraid? Because I love her? Because I am curious.

Curiosity killed the cat, my mother likes to say. It was her way of shutting me up, warning me that too many questions would lead to dangerous truths.

My daughter is heavy. Heavier than she has ever been before. Heavy like picking up an adult. Her body soft but also like a sack of potatoes.

"I show," she says and nuzzles her face to my neck. I wonder if I smell like my mother did. "Down," she says next, so I set her down on the floor amongst her discarded teeth and watch her gather them. She piles them high, builds a wobbly structure that peaks like a tent or a teepee.

I hear the back door open and slam shut. Dillon is inside. Thing One and Two are with him. They chatter. I imagine their hands full of fruit and veggies.

"Honey!" my husband calls. "The rice is burning. Jesus!"

He is annoyed. Annoyed because I burned the rice. Annoyed because I walked away from the burning rice. He's still clueless. So unaware of what I am. Of what we've made.

In the kitchen, my husband asks my eldest to find me.

Lucia stands on stubby legs, leaving her little sculpture on the floor to walk herself to the bedroom door and shut it, before turning back to me to say, "Lock, please." I rise and move to the door to follow her instructions. Then she says, "I. Me. More."

"*You* are more?" I ask. A shiver vibrates my spine.

"I you," Lucia says. "And you me. *We* more."

PART II

Wean

When I was five years old, I attacked a little girl at school. I hadn't remembered the incident until just now. Lucia has dredged it up in me. I still don't fully remember the "attack" part, only the meeting afterward where my feet hung off the edge of a too-tall chair and Principal Franklin, rings of sweat under both her armpits and her hair disheveled, presumably from my antics, told me and my mother that we would need to "seek another institution for any future educational endeavors."

"It's public school. You can't expel her," my mother says. I can tell from her wavering tone that she doesn't know if this is true.

"We have a no-tolerance policy here," the principal says. Her voice is shaky. Her hands too. One of her bright pink press-on nails is missing.

"A no-tolerance policy? For what? Children?"

"For violence. It's very clearly laid out in the handbook, which you signed off on."

"But it's kindergarten!"

"I'm well aware of what grade your daughter is in. I'm sorry, but she *attacked* that little girl," the principal says to my mother.

She clears her voice and I see her notice her missing nail before she puts her hands in her lap behind her desk where we can't see.

I'm only five years old, but even I can see that Mrs. Franklin isn't sorry. I can tell by the way she's pressing both her palms into her desk, so strong that she might push right through the metal.

"I find that hard to believe," my mother says. "She's just a little girl. Small for her age even. How much harm could a sweet little girl do?"

My mother has shown up in her best pantsuit and her hair is pulled back into a low pony. It's her "professional" outfit, the one she uses for interviews. It used to work. Used to get her jobs, but not lately. Lately, the outfit looks old, and her hair is greasy, like stringy greasy.

We've been living in our car for so many days that I can't remember them all, but she could have showered at the YWCA like we sometimes do. She smells funny, like cigarettes and armpits. I bet Mrs. Franklin has never once forgotten to put on her deodorant before work or even tried a cigarette.

I wish with my whole body that my mother hadn't come. I sat here alone for ninety-seven minutes—I know because I watched the clock on the wall count each second off.

Don't come, don't come, don't, don't, don't, I chanted in my head. I could handle this on my own. Like I handled everything. My mother would make it worse. If she didn't show up, I could wait out the day, then get on the bus like usual. Mrs. Franklin would feel so bad for me that she would let the whole thing go.

Then Mama showed up pissed off and smelly and now she's arguing with Mrs. Franklin when she shouldn't. I did a bad thing. I got mad and things went dark and now I'm here.

I stare at the toothpaste stain on my skirt that looks like a smiley face—it's been there for a couple weeks. We only have money for laundry once a month, so I've got a ways to go.

"I'm sure the other family will share the photos of their daughter's injuries if you want to escalate this. I will tell you that I spent the better part of an hour talking them down from calling the cops. Do you want that?"

"What's the family's name?" my mother demands.

"You know I can't share that."

"That girl provoked Thea."

"Thea, is that true?" Mrs. Franklin tries to use her calm voice with me, but she sounds shaky. Why does she sound shaky? Is she scared of my mom? Of me?

I swing my feet harder, let my sneakers hit loudly on the legs of the wooden chair.

"Sweetie, tell us what happened from your perspective," my mom says.

I've been silent so long that speaking out loud seems impossible. My throat is sore from whatever I did, an event I can't quite remember but know was bad.

"Don't know," I croak.

"Of course you know!" Now my mom is yelling at me, and I want to cry. I do cry, but I do it real quiet, like an adult.

"Thea," my mother says in a stern voice. She thinks saying my name will make me obey, but I'm too embarrassed. I got so angry when Gretchen shoved me. I should tell them about how last week she chewed up a hard-boiled egg and spit it in my backpack or how she hid her poopy underwear in my cubby. I should tell them that she likes to pinch me. I could show them the purple bruises that look like little flowers all over my arms.

"It's okay, Thea," Principal Franklin says to me. I don't believe her, but I can tell some of her sympathy has shifted toward me. She looks back at my mom. "Your daughter had a terrible day, and I have to say that there are so many witnesses to the incident that we are going to have to provide emotional support not only to the little girl she assaulted but also to the rest of the class and the staff. It was . . . traumatic."

I catch a wild flash of myself as I reach out for Gretchen's hair and twist it in my fist so tight that I can yank her straight down to the ground with it. The growl of my glee now feels embarrassing. Shameful, like I ran around the school naked and now everyone knows all my parts.

"You saw it?" my mother asks, as if she's just found the loophole. Like Mrs. Franklin is a liar and pointing that out will solve everything.

"I only came in at the end, but a teacher saw the whole thing."

I bit my teacher, I think and wrap my arms over the hurt in my tummy. I remember the way her arm felt between my two hands. How I held her like a corncob and bit right into the inside softness of her forearm. I remember too how good it felt while I was biting. Blood like butter.

"Ohhhh," I say. A groan that comes out like vomit. I clap one hand over my mouth to stop more sounds.

"You have something to say, sweetie?" my mom asks. She doesn't call me sweetie, and it makes me feel worse. Fake. Like I'm not even me.

I shake my head no.

"The teacher was hurt separating the girls. She's headed to the emergency room, actually. I'll have to share that *something* happened if asked by the next school, but I can avoid sharing that Thea's a biter. It's not a label she'll want to carry forward because biting, well, schools take that seriously."

"Oh, please," my mother says waving at Mrs. Franklin.

"The bite marks are quite deep, actually, but the teacher is willing to not press charges if you get Thea some help."

"Help? What kind of help? A dentist?"

My body goes cold and my legs still. I love my teacher. Why would I do that?

When we are done, my mother drags me to the car by one of my bruised arms and yells at me the whole drive back to that ABQ apartment with the barred windows.

"You want us to be homeless forever?" she asks. "You need to learn to get yourself under control. I've given you all the skills you need to be better and you're not using them. You have to want to be normal. Nobody needs to see the full you, Thea. You need to bury that behavior deep until you forget it was even there."

I sit in the hot car and feel how right she was about me. My jaw aches with my own evil, and even as the door opens to that dark, slender terror of a man, I know I am old enough to know better. That I am the ruined one.

After that, I learned how to put on my own foot brace at night. I tied the bandana tighter after my mother fell asleep. I weaned myself of childhood and stepped away from anything that felt like need. I was entirely and utterly on my own, and I refused to fuck it all up again. So, when the bad things happened—the ones that came in ALL CAPS—I said nothing. I didn't ask for help. I ran dialogue in my head of what I would say and what she would say, and I'd come up with what needed to be done or not done. I handled *it*—no matter what *it* was. *It* was, after all, in some small or large part my fault. "It takes two to tango," my mother loved to say.

⌄ ⌄

I blink myself back into the room with Lucia. My daughter has brought this memory out of me. Pulled it into the present with her evil grin.

I think too of Jeremy, now five, and realize how small I must have been. My heart and brain soft and tiny and sad. How could anyone expect a child to see and feel such horribly adult things? How could my mother have looked at me and thought: *She's got this.*

And, suddenly, I wonder, *Did I have this family just to spite my mother?*

Maybe I never wanted them at all, my spite family. Did I birth them for show? Jeremy first, who looks more like my husband than me, then Sebastian. Did I feel gratified by my mother's rejection of him? A kind of: *See, I told you my mother was horrible. She doesn't even love her own grandson.* And, as if to finish proving my point, I bore Lucia—the biggest and baddest of them all.

Time in the real world, in the right now, is measured by the sounds of the rising panic of my little spiteless or spiteful family. Most of them remain locked on the other side of the kids' bedroom door. My husband's hesitant knocks speed up. He hollers. His fear scares our two normal children—the two that are on his side. The doorknob rattles. His shoulder hits thick pine. The bang does nothing to move the door, but he tries again anyway. Again, and again, and again. It makes me feel terrible because I can hear he is truly upset, but it makes Lucia giggle, so I focus on the absurd fact that if anyone knows the door cannot be broken down it should be the man who hung it. But men have been raised to believe they can kick down doors. Lucia laughs at him, and I find, although reluctantly, that I like the sound of Lucia's mischievous giggle. The tiny gleam in her gorgeous eyes.

"Pow! Pow!" I say and punch my fists into the air between us as if we are in a comic book panel and I am a man chopping down a door with my bare hands. She laughs harder, a delicious giggle.

Sweet Sebastian has long ago begun to cry. He's what I hear when our laughter dies down. He sounds like he can't get enough air—breath hees and haws out of him, like he's imitating a donkey. The sharp pain this sends through my heart makes me gasp. Dillon tries to calm him; I listen appreciatively to his soft, fatherly voice that does nothing to calm our son. He's a good father. He loves them. He talks to them. Shows them how to do things with a patience I don't have. Dillon's father is a good father. Wise and calm and interested. It's passed down, I suppose, the skill of parenting, which means, of course, that I don't have it.

My husband shushes Sebastian next, kindly at first, then unkindly—neither of which works on Sebastian's breathless fear. Jeremy can be heard next. My sweet eldest swooping in to save the day.

"Daddy," Sebastian says. "You're scary to me."

Good, I think. *He's scary. Not me. I win.* Testosterone always raises its ugly, spermy head.

"S'okay, baby brother. S'okay," Jeremy says.

I imagine him rubbing circles on his little brother's back. Those circles are getting tighter and tighter.

I keep my focus on Lucia. Her little eyes dance with light—a merriment that does not wane and seems to say, *Look what we can do, Mommy! We can hurt them all, every single one!*

I hear whispering amid the other-side-of-the-door crying, and soon little Jeremy is pressing his mouth to the keyhole.

"Mama," he says. "Please open. I need you."

My husband has put him up to this, which allows me to ignore the pull on my heart and gravitate to anger. Anger is always safer. Rage is a woman's superpower. It makes me forget that Dillon is human. That he is kind. It pushes away my empathy. What kind of father cannot comfort his own children? Get to his own wife? Save his smallest baby girl from whatever madness he thinks has her locked inside this room? What kind of weak, trivial man sends in his oldest son to beg and manipulate? *I knew it,* my mind hisses. *I knew he was worthless.*

There were so many men in my childhood—the one who brushed my hair, the one on the other side of the shower curtain, the one who slept naked, the one who couldn't remember my name, the one who drank too much, and the one who didn't drink at all. The one who brought his son to live with us, a tween who pissed on my best stuffies and drew a huge, unerasable dick on my bedroom wall.

There were so, so many. And, when there weren't any, there was me and a mother and the shadow of whomever she would bring home next. Without a man in the house, she cried too much and slept too much. I was chronically invisible or too visible. She relied on me too much when there wasn't a man around. Clung to me. I lost the few friends I had in those months—like a teenage girl with her first boyfriend, I lost track of everyone but my mother.

Men, even the evilest, always believe themselves to be the hero. In that whole list of Mama's boyfriends, there was never an exception. They ride in to save the day, and if there is nothing to save you from, they beat you down first so they can ease the throttling pain. Like my mother, they like you best when they've got you exhausted from childrearing and the heat and down a dirt road no one likes to travel.

"Thea! This is absurd!" I can hear Dillon's fear—it makes the same sound as his anger—and he is scrambling, losing ground. It rarely occurs to men that the world is five seconds away from being out of their control, so when the shit hits the fan, they don't know what to do.

"Maaammmmmaaaa," Sebastian wails.

It almost works, but I do not answer. I sit on the ground with Lucia and let my breasts fill with milk. I thought I'd already willfully and successfully dried up, but hearing the despair makes my body respond to Sebastian.

"Get him out of here," Dillon hollers at Jeremy. "Please," he offers next and kindlier.

He wants him to take his brother somewhere else, since his wails haven't won me over, and I think, *Where? Fool.* This house he's built for us is too small for any greater division than the one I've already achieved.

My body continues to ache from the need of and for my children, but I do not move. I stay on the floor with Lucia. Lucia and I are locked into each other.

"I'm serious, Thea. You're scaring me," my husband says. "Are you hurt? Open the door or I'll take it off the hinges. It's your choice," my husband says.

I soften to his plea, think about unlocking the door. I feel sorry for this man who married me. This man who thought fathering children with me would equal a life well lived. Men are told life will be easy. Simple. They will get what they want, and if they don't, they will kick down some motherfuckin' doors! Poor, sweet boy.

Dillon's family is large and sprinkled throughout Albuquerque. It's a fucking gaggle and he speaks fondly of every single one, knowing fully that some of them are trash.

"Family is all we have," he says. It's an adage he passes on to our children, and every time he says it, I feel a little sick. If family is all I have, I better start taking better care of the one I've made, because the one I was born to sucked ass.

I used to tell myself that if I told my mother how much I hurt, she would care. She would be sad and sorry, and she would hold me and apologize.

I told her once that I was upset that she didn't stand up for me more when I was a little girl.

She scoffed and said, "You don't know how good you had it."

"Are you serious?" I asked and laughed, thinking this a joke—how could she make dark times even darker with one short sentence?

She said, "You don't know horrible. *My* mother was horrible.

She never saw me for who I was. Never hugged me or told me she loved me. She was high most of my childhood."

"High on what?" I asked.

"How could that possibly matter?" my mom asked, as if my desire for details was repulsive.

"Okay, Mom," I said. "Never mind."

One small exchange with my mother has the power to exhaust me.

Having my own daughter has made a funny thing happen for me. While the boys taught me busyness and play and forgiveness, Lucia is bringing the memories, and with them the rage, giving it all voice and volume, making me see what I must have looked like. I too was a baby. A toddler. A very little girl. The puffy pads of my toes once looked like a puppy's tiny toe-beans and my earlobes were soft slivers of skin covered in largely invisible, blond hairs. It is becoming harder and harder to fathom how I was raised. You, their mother, are their everything. Their everyone. And how could someone so small, so sweet, be at fault, be ignored?

My husband interrupts my selfishness. He says, "Thea, I know you've been hurting more than you've let on. I can see it. I've been waiting for you to tell me, but I see now that I should have made you tell me."

An alarm goes off in my head. He's noticed I'm different. He's seen *me*? I did not know. Did not notice. How could I not know he was looking? I remember that long-ago teacher that I sent to the hospital. Had she seen me? What I was? What I am?

"Do you need me to get a friend out here? Maybe call your mother?"

"My mother? Don't be ridiculous," I say.

It's not Dillon's fault. I don't talk about my past. Not with him. Not with anybody. It's part of why it was so alarming to hear that Tori thought she knew something about my mother. Hell, I don't remember much of my own childhood, so I couldn't possibly share it with other people. Much of that time has been sucked into a black hole of best-forgotten things. And, like a closet door accidentally left open a crack, you must keep your eyes on the dark space beyond it just in case it's finally the hour, the minute when something gruesome crawls out to eat you.

Still, Dillon should know better than to invoke my mother's name. He knows her.

"I'm sorry, Thea. I shouldn't have suggested that your mother would somehow help this situation. I know she isn't helpful. I'm just trying to understand . . . to get you to tell me what's wrong."

"Call her if you want," I say. "It's not like she'll come out here anyway."

Lucia senses my sadness, bunches her pretty little eyebrows together with concern.

"My mother doesn't love me," I say to her and only her, and the rage I've been trying to wean myself of rushes through me, more powerful than it has ever been before. "But I love you," I say to Lucia with determination. "I do love you and I will love you. I won't be afraid. No matter what."

"Thea, this is crazy. Please. What's going on?"

"Nothing is going on. Just leave us alone."

"I can't do that, Thea. Lucia, sweetie, you okay? Do you need Daddy?"

She grins at me and says nothing.

"Good girl," I whisper to Lucia. Then to Dillon I say, "Can you go find Lilibeth?" I figure this will keep him busy. The walk to her house, wrangling the boys there and back. A little time. That's all I need. And, as expected, he jumps at the chance to do something useful. To push toward a solve.

I hear them out there finding shoes.

"We'll be back, sweetie," Dillon says through the door, and I wonder if this "sweetie" is for me or Lucia. "Thea, I found these at the bottom of that photo box. I don't think you saw them. Maybe they'll make you feel better?" He sounds so unsure that I feel bad for him. "I think you took them a long time ago. I think they're how you saw the world back then and that's something, right? Different from all the other things in that box?"

I don't answer.

"Okay then. I'm trusting you two alone together." He tries out a lighthearted laugh, but it's fake and ends too abruptly. "I'll slide them under the door. We'll be back with Lilibeth soon, and we can all hang out. Talk. Figure out what it is you need, Thea." I think I can hear him put his palm to the door. "I love you girls," he says, and I bite my tongue to keep from responding. I am a cruel, cruel bitch.

A manila envelope slides under the door and glides to my hip. I hear the back door slap shut behind them.

We honeymooned in Puerto Rico, Dillon and me. We stayed in San Juan, but my favorite days were spent hiking in El Yunque. I'd never been to a tropical rainforest. A place so wet with waterfalls that the air felt thick. So different from my desert home that it felt like magic, just being there. My skin softened. I forgot about lotion, neglected my Nalgene bottle of water. My dry eyes ceased their itching. Another couple told us there was a space behind one of those falls. A hollow where you could stand behind water, so we waded in, Dillon and me. Dillon, confident as always, disappeared gracefully behind the thick stream and into the carved space. He was gone less than a minute and came out smoothly.

He said, "It's easy!"

So, I went in. I held my breath. The water poured down on me so fast and so hard that I panicked. Turned, twisted. Let my breath out and the water in. I could not find the hollow space, and I could not find the fresh air I'd come from. The world was only water, and it filled my mouth, flooded my tunnels. And just when I thought I'd drown, I felt this powerful urge to roar, to open my body up wider, as if letting all the elements in would save me. So, I did. I flared up with anger, with energy. I gargled that waterfall, took it all in as if I were the more powerful thing. I felt like a lioness. It's hard to describe, but I went from flailing to rising.

But then, my husband was reaching in and pulling me out. He'd come to the rescue. I hid the disappointment I felt about not rescuing myself. It had felt like a big, great thing inside me was about to present itself, and Dillon's reach had stopped it. I settled back into myself, framed my face into a smile. The weight of that water and how my body conquered it for the briefest of moments matches this rage. This heavy, heavy anger that I've been so close to drowning in my whole fucking life. Can I turn it into something powerful? Vengeful?

I try. The rage waterfalls through me, takes my breath from my lungs, but Lucia stops me from suffocating with a smile. Her teeth thicker and brighter and sharper than any human being's should ever be, and she says, "In. Let in."

"What will you do?" I ask.

It is a calm question. I do not know why I ask it. Maybe I just want to hear more of her voice.

"Devour," she says.

It is a big word for a baby. And I take the word choice seriously. It is a word that implies deep hunger. A word that evokes speed and purpose. She opens her jaw, wide and toothful, and inside I imagine a bloody mess. Dillon and Jeremy and Sebastian piled up like logs inside her throat. Their bodies bloodied; their limbs mixed into a single fucking disaster.

"Let's not," I say.

I'm frightened but also intrigued. It's the feeling of wonder that childhood used to offer. That feeling of *What will happen next?* And, *Am I brave enough?* A feeling that always brought giddiness even as it led down a path to dread.

The fantasy of hurting those who hurt me as a child peeks out from behind Lucia's many, many teeth.

"You will too," Lucia says, and the word she spoke before echoes in my brain in a new and dreadful way: *DEVOUR*. "You've begun," she says.

"I haven't and I won't," I say in my best not-right-now-young-lady voice, but it rattles me. This idea that I was devoured long ago and that my spite has been hungrier than I thought. What have I done? I mean, beyond making more little people to feed to the world. Producing boys that will become men and step into a world that will offer them too much while telling them they are welcome to take the rest by force.

I pick up the envelope now. Its belly is full with photos, if my husband is right. I flip open the gummy flap and dump the contents between me and Lucia. It stops my breath. Image after image of houses. Photographs *I* took with my Polaroid, back in the day. The memories flood back.

Lucia begins to arrange them on the floor in a little quilted square just as I'd once done as a teenager, when I taped them to my bedroom wall.

"What these?" she asks.

I squeeze my eyes shut, make the dark darker and remember what I haven't remembered in a long time. Is it a good memory? A bad one? Perhaps there is no such thing. No distinction, just a jabberwocky of garbage and grace.

Here are the photographs to go with each and every open

house and estate sale my mother and I ever visited. Usually, they were on Sundays, so they became a sort of church for us. I worshipped at the altar of these dreamy spaces. Sometimes they were sad, full of dead people stuff. Everything, I mean everything, had a price tag, and those price tags made me hopeful. It meant that even the shittiest of things could hold value. I loved the idea that I could craft what people saw. Sell the best image of myself. Angle it so that it was no longer trash but easily treasure.

My mother encouraged my longing. We'd play together. Discuss loudly where we'd put our future sofa (we did not have a sofa but rather a futon on an old metal frame). Express how sad it made us that anyone would paint over such lovely hardwood. We talked to the house as we went through. Or, at least, that's what I thought we were doing.

I was fifteen when my mother told me that she stole from the houses we saw. Not just extra cookies but money from top drawers. Jewelry left tableside. Lingerie, T-shirts, piggy banks. We were in the bathroom of a large Pueblo-Spanish revival, and I was pretending to do my makeup in the mirror. The makeup was from the top drawer. It belonged to the homeowner, so I, of course, didn't apply it. I left the lid on the mascara and mimed it brushing my lashes. When I set it down, my mother broke the moment by shoving it in her pocket, then opening the cabinet and stuffing her purse with the homeowner's medication.

"What are you doing?" I asked. The sinking feeling in my

stomach was always there, but I did such a good job ignoring it that I was surprised when it sank deeper.

"What I always do," she said, not registering my alarm.

"Always?"

"Of course," she said, and shut the medicine cabinet.

My real reflection stared back at me, my complexion yellowed, greasy. I turned my eyes toward her in the mirror.

"What did you think we were doing here?" she asked.

Embarrassment rushed through me. So thick and red that it felt like my body was evacuating itself.

I thought we were there for the same reason—my mother and I—for the love of the space, the dream of belonging. I always took my camera for an exterior shot of the front of each house just like I had taken a picture of every apartment entrance where we'd ever lived—I was always trying to find a home. When we had money to develop the film and I had my own room, I'd add the picture to the quilt of possibilities on the wall. I was collecting futures while my mom robbed them.

That night I ripped all the photographs off my bedroom wall and stuffed them in a manila envelope. Tucked them away and forgot about them until Dillon slid them under the door.

Lucia and I re-create my past on the floor with the photographs from the envelope. We do it with care, and she points at them. Giggles at some. Marvels at others. I do not tell her the memories. The good or the bad, but she seems to see me in these photos. To get enough of a story from seeing what I saw.

"We go here, now," Lucia says, pointing her finger at the photo of that first apartment. Even in the photo, the barred window keeps the dark in.

"How?" I ask Lucia.

"We go through. In," she says. "We fix."

I almost tell her there is no going back. There is no fixing the past, only pushing forward as fast as you can to build a new reality, but is that the lesson I should teach my child? Should she plow forward heedlessly until the day something stops her in her tracks and she breaks down like I have? Or should she focus inward and deny, deny, deny like my mother has? Or should she do her own thing? Look at the past. Attack it. Adjust it.

Instead of arguing, I trust her. I put my hand over her hand on the image and the room around us changes, becomes elastic and pink until we are traveling back into my past, to the time and place of this photograph.

We move in a warm darkness, a soft tunnel of pinkish-brown material that turns spongy. It eases closer to my shoulders, touches the top of my head. We are in a round tube that reminds me of the collapsible play tube we bought for the kids—Dillon loved to drop it over his body and chase them around the house, reaching out for them from the top until they disappeared into the big rainbow worm with him. They loved it.

This tunnel is thicker and darker than that accordion of a toy, and it has a heartbeat. The thick of it throbs around us. Three strings of heat that press in. In then out. In then out. A heartbeat. A breath. A pulse.

"Lucia," I say, but the name comes out an echo of another time. A memory of a sound that maybe only I hear. The tunnel reddens, thickens. Becomes . . .

Umbilical, I think.

We crawl forward. Shimmying around each other. Twisting and braiding. I recall that not only does the umbilical cord feed the baby—nutrients float from mother to baby—but stuff flows the other way too. What the baby doesn't need, can't use, goes back to the mother. Rejected. Does that make Lucia and me food or feces? The thought makes me smile.

I know what I am. The discard. The stanky pile no one needs. But that isn't Lucia. I've mistaken her for evil, for something sloughed off. I was wrong, and this makes me laugh, makes me wonder if I might be wrong about myself too.

Suddenly, I get a whiff of moth balls and leaking air conditioners and moldy cloth shower curtains. It smells like animal pelts and motor oil. Like the Bosque River when it is too low. I hear Aspen leaves whoosh as Lucia drops out of sight ahead of me.

I keep crawling, the world around me pinkens into red, tightening further until it can't tighten any more, and I'm falling. Falling into a darker place where there is no sound.

I fall for a long time. I feel all alone. Empty. No monstrous daughter. No anger. Only the dark remains as company. I think of Lewis Carroll's *Through the Looking-Glass and What Alice Found There*—my daughter appears briefly in the dark with a Cheshire grin and buttons for eyes. My mother looks as if the Queen of Hearts mated with the Bandersnatch—a bearlike creature in a red-and-black dress, a tiny crown on her head and claws long enough to off with my head.

I land softly on a patch of fake grass.

I am in a big, dark space that is lightening as I sit, little plastic blades of green poking my calves and ankles. Spotlights brighten overhead, and I see that Lucia is here too. I stand. I take her hand as we watch the mass of buildings before us come to light.

The structure in front of me is the Scotch-taped image that Lucia and I just puzzled together, brought to life. The mosaic that was once taped to my wall. A mishmash of places known and wished for. On my wall, they looked like a quilt, a colorful rendering of a life I longed to live. Dreamy and hopeful and well placed, each photograph complementing the next. It was beautiful. Brought to life like this, it is something else. A Frankenstein construction of a forgotten past. Something stitched together. Literally. Large black threads weave one house into the next, as if a giant has brought fat thread and a sharp needle to the party and made sure no house can live separate from another. Memories attached painfully to each other in an irrevocable way. It's like something out of a horror movie—we are standing on Elm Street looking in at the nightmare, and if we go farther in, will we ever come back out?

The structure goes so high and wide, I cannot see its beginnings or its endings. The stitching is as thick as cable, a running base stitch that has bitten from the skin of each house to the next. The spots where that needle must've pierced look raw, punctured, thousands of little wounds pulled tight. I realize that my past is made of haunted houses—Amityville after Amityville quilted together to make an even bigger space in which to keep ghosts.

"This feels like a bad idea," I say to Lucia.

She spreads her lips wide, and I see that her teeth have vampired, sharpened further to stabby little points that are too big for needlework and too deadly for a little girl's mouth. Lucia is a weapon, and a weapon doesn't care who it hurts. She's lost baby fat, grown more skeletal. In this world of horror houses, she is leathery, bat-like.

She gestures for me to follow, and I stare at the back of her neck. It looks longer somehow, her spine in harsh relief on her back. Her hair hangs loose against her shoulder blades—two little wings of bone just under her soft skin, sharp enough to slice her open. To slice me open. She is both delicate and fierce, dangerous for sure.

She walks me forward to a barred window—the one I know too well—and I watch as she reaches for the bars and pulls them open, right to left, like a kitchen cupboard, before she attaches her hands and feet to the stucco and scuttles up and in—a girl gone cockroach, then gone altogether.

I follow. My body doing what her body shows me it can do. I feel roachy. Uncrushable and fast.

Lucia and I stand side by side in a bathtub. The faucet drips. A sound that I forgot I remembered. The porcelain under my feet is a familiar yellow that one can easily tell is meant to be white. The cloth shower curtain in front of me has no liner—it never did. It smells of mold. It is stuck to the tub; its bottom edge coated in the sort of scum you get when you don't clean your fish tank. I become aware of the tight feeling in my stomach that lived in my abdomen as a child. A knot of nervousness that could rush up my throat or out my bottom at any moment. I thought they had gone away—all those feelings—but they are all still here, as full and grotesque as ever. I hate it, this feeling of weakness. Of collapsibility. It lives so comfortably inside my guts that I had forgotten to notice it. I feel its thumping life force; its beating heart causes constant terror, but then I feel Lucia's hand in mine. The soft smallness of her makes me mad at that knot of tension in my gut. What little girl could possibly deserve this big of a feeling?

Lucia holds my gaze. She keeps her vampiric shark smile closed, and although the sheer width of her lips gives away the secret just waiting to spread underneath, she looks almost normal. Simply beautiful. Simply sweet. As if it is possible that she is no more complicated than what is on her surface.

But then a shadow comes.

On the other side of the curtain.

The biggest, oldest monster of them all.

The sick in my insides squirms and worms. The boil of it threatens to find its way out—my body has never felt more vulnerable, more perforated. The monster on the other side of the curtain is man-sized.

He clears his throat. It's a sound I remember so well. He made so many noises. Gurgles and gargles and roars. He blows his nose, spits in the bathroom sink, farts. How can a body make so much noise? It is morning, and in the morning, he is always at his loudest. He is grumpy and regretful and the clearing away of yesterday's mistakes is so guttural that it makes my own insides begin to rumble and tumble.

Next, he takes a piss. Urine hits water—not entirely, of course, because I will later wipe drops off the seat that he has neglected to lift so that the hot little bits of him do not burn on the skin of my thighs and butt for the rest of the day. The hot smell is nauseating. He does not care that I am in the shower. That I am getting ready for school. Later I will begin showering before he is home from work, which could be eight p.m. or five p.m. or three p.m. If it is three, he is home first and my shower is not safe no matter when I take it, so I go for morning, thinking maybe he will sleep in, maybe he will sleep, maybe he will . . .

Before I know the pattern, the first time, I say, "Hello."

I say it when he opens the bathroom door. I heard the opening and shutting but no answer from him. It is that first time when I peek. I part the curtain just to confirm that it's him—

even though I know it is by his noise and his shadow—and I don't want him to be embarrassed, because he clearly doesn't know that I'm in here even though the shower makes a whining noise when it runs and the bathroom somehow fills up superfast with hot steam even though the water itself doesn't stay hot for as long as I need it to. I part the curtain, and he is wiping his mouth clear of his sink-spitting event and looking right back at me, as if he knows where my eyes will be at all times and that's when I make my seven-year-old mistake.

I look down. I look to see if he is naked. I look to see a penis, because I've never seen one before. I am curious until I am not. Then I am regretful, and I know for the rest of the times this happens, that it is in some part my fault because I looked. The pink sausage of a thing sits on a wrinkly bed of skin that looks lopsided. I stare too long, and the thing swells, peeks back at me until I pull the shower curtain shut and freeze. Stand like the deer my mom and I almost hit in the road when we were coming back from the foothills. I couldn't understand that deer. The way it just stood and stared. It would have kept still as we ran right into it. I didn't understand until I was seven and behind that curtain.

I shiver but otherwise do not move.

I haven't thought about him or his hideous fucking cock in a long time. It's not that I ever forgot him. No. I remember him well, but I spent so much time in my twenties sleeping with men, trying to get a view of a different penis to erase that first one that

I thought maybe I'd at least rendered him unmemorable. I haven't.

The grand, grody details of him are present again, right here. Front and center. And I feel small.

The smell of mildew combined with the rank stench of his morning piss is so thick that it colors the steam a sickly green. The sounds of his heels bounce on linoleum. He is shaking the last drops off his cock. He does another hocking spit—I'd forgotten this one—into the toilet to top off the rest before flushing it all away. The water runs like ice from the showerhead and never fully recovers from that flush. This I remember.

Now there are two of us in the shower. Lucia and me. The shadow looms larger as his noises cease. I smell beer. I hear him rub the stubble on his own face. I stand as still as I can. The water is already cold, but I do nothing to speed up my shower. I don't, after all, quite know why we're here. I look at Lucia, thinking I should protect her from this, but she grins sharklike at me, and I see that she could swallow me whole if she chose to. Her eyes bulge hungrily out of her; pupils tiny inside huge white orbs that look like marbles readying to spill out and shoot across the ground.

It used to end with a grunt, then the sound of him washing his hands for at least five minutes. Getting soap at least twice. The water turned to ice before he left. The shampoo in my hair was harder to wash out, leading the other second graders to make fun of me.

I used to curl up on the bottom of the bathtub, thinking

perhaps if he can't see me, the ritual will stop, but it was naïve. There was no amount of small that would make this stop. I knew this. I learned this. And yet, somehow, I also know that it is my fault. And fault lasts a lifetime.

I look away from the shadow and down to my daughter-thing. Water rises around our legs. Cold water. The yellow tub wrinkles under the waves of the rising tide and the edge of the shower curtain soaks itself in the muck. I look closer at monstrous little Lucia, who is peeling my hands away from her face and letting her lips part.

"Watch, Mama," she says, as if we are at the swimming pool, and she is going to sit crisscross applesauce at the bottom of the pool.

Like any good mom, I watch. I watch as she crawls over the edge of the tub to situate herself on the bathroom floor—the shower curtain still between them, shielding all but his ankles. First, she cracks her mouth wide and wider still, as if readying her jaw muscles for the work ahead. Next, she makes her mouth smaller. With her lips pursed, she presses her cheek to the floor; she's fixed her mouth as if around a large straw, and his leg hairs respond first, pull toward her mouth like she's a vacuum cleaner. Once Lucia has the attention of his plethora of leg hair, his skin comes next. It stretches toward her like dirty Silly Putty until it is pulling painfully away from his muscles. Ripping to show a brighter pink underneath. Ligaments glisten once revealed and next comes bone. I am reminded of the nights we buy a roasted chicken from the grocery and drop it in the middle of the table, so we can all pull meat from it as we wish. Napkins in our laps to clear the grease between pulls.

She skins him from the feet up with seemingly no effort at all. Only his screams tell us it is a painful process. His pitch rises as the layers of him disappear, his sweet internal organs losing purchase as his bones pile then slide down Lucia's ever-expanding throat.

There is a crunching, a grinding, a calamari squeak that must be his teeth on her teeth on teeth, then she turns to me grinning, blood on her chin.

"All done," she says, and the gulp of her throat takes the shape of the man that I once thought was too big for life.

My insides feel different. Something hurts just a little less. He isn't dead, dead. What happened still happened. I remember it. More clearly than ever actually, but the feeling of shame has somehow lessened. Lucia has digested the secrecy of it. Her body is processing it, breaking it down into more sizable bits, and there is suddenly room behind my breasts. My heart beats loud with life. My rage has always lived in my rib cage. I picture my insides stuck sharp with the dense mat of a desert plant called a goathead. Those little weedy plants thrive in the heat. They start off flowering, looking harmless right up until the point that they grow dry and spiky with devil heads, their sharp horns piercing bike tires and shoes and feet. I picture them inside me. Their horns dug into places I can't ever reach. But now, one seems to have rocked loose, dropped into the acid of my stomach perhaps, destroyed. One tiny spot of my insides suddenly clear of pain.

"Oh," I say.

The monster knot of sharp inside me grows rumbly again. There is still plenty of embarrassment. Shame pokes at the muscles between my ribs. Threatens my lungs.

"Again?" Lucia asks. She is eager, as if requesting another push on the swings.

"Again," I say, and feel my own shark smile spread across my face.

"And again," she says.

"And again."

Lucia claps her little hands together in glee.

With the man swallowed and the shower curtain gone, ahead of us is the door out of the bathroom and into the living room of the apartment. I step out of the tub first and turn to lift Lucia. My feet squelch on a soaked bath mat.

I open the bathroom door, and on the other side, there is the dark living room I remember too well. It smells of my mother's perfume. It smells of peanut butter toast and the hot electric buzz of my old television. The television is on—the fuzz of its screen lighting the dark room. The floor is crummy, gritty with outside sand that never gave up coming in. It was my first home. The first I remember anyway. Inside the memory, I feel my little child body pressed to the floor—belly to ground and bony elbows digging into fake wood, my knuckles propping up my head. The back of my neck aches, but I ignore it. I bounce the tops of my feet off the floor, one leg then the other, until my mother hollers from the bedroom, "Hush, Thea!"

I look to my mother's open bedroom door. It gapes back at me like a rectangular version of the well from *The Ring*. The deep black of that mouth of a space looks like it could take shape, grow teeth and claws, slash me open. My fear beads up on my skin. I'm sweating as I picture the scariest villain in recent memory crawling out of that television. Samara Morgan's limbs origami toward us; her long dark hair is matted with tumbleweeds. Her face, her intentions so well hidden until the very last moment that all we can do is stare until the full extent of our pain ravages our bones. Wakes us to her hunger. The dark becomes unstoppable. It comes for every one of us.

The goatheads poke their little warnings at my heart.

Lucia and I walk through the dark pit of the bedroom door, and we find ourselves at my mother's bedside. We are looking down at my mother and the same boyfriend—the one Lucia ate. It's funny, because if pressed, I would have said it was a different man, a different boyfriend, but I see now that this slumbering man is one and the same. The room is dark. It smells dank. There are dirty glasses on the bedside table. A pipe meant for a substance I try not to guess and a lighter with the pink head of a Playboy Bunny on the front. I watch the hand of the man reach across my mother so that he can touch the little girl sleeping there. He strokes her back, her butt.

Is my mother really asleep?

Her snoring proves she is as she snorts and turns over. He moves his hand to her back to settle her, as if he'd meant to be there on her all along.

Lucia wrinkles her brow, staring up at me, as if to ask permission to get started.

"My mother could have protected me," I say. "She was too busy paying attention to herself to know I needed help." But then I feel the bigger realization that my mother wasn't just being passive or ignorant. She was using me. I was the buffer between her and her men. A shield. This knowledge makes the pokeys inside me grow bigger, but their swell is temporary.

I purposely forgot the things that happened to me when I was supposedly in my mother's care. First, I made them into figments of my imagination, so they wouldn't seem so scary, so real. Then I blocked them entirely. I kept myself safe for years and years by pretending the big, bad man never existed.

"Do it," I say to Lucia, and Lucia takes hold of his foot and starts to chew. He screams. He thrashes. He reaches for us, hoping to pull me in with him. The shame of his touch fights to stay strong in me but loses.

Lucia fits his whole calf into her mouth. His torso. She reaches his shoulder, then moves down to his elbow. She bites that reachy, lookie-loo mitt of a hand neatly free from the once-there rest of him. The hand flops off the bed and onto the floor. Blood squirts.

The room is splattered with him. When Lucia is done, it rains down over sleepy mommy and girl. Soaks us. It sprays the popcorn ceiling of the room.

"More?" Lucia asks. "Finish?"

I see his head still there on the bed, and it reminds me of poor, decapitated Alex Forrest, her beak of a mouth open and closing as Lucia played with her remains. He will be dead soon.

"Leave it," I say. "Pain cures all wounds." It's a saying I've just made up, but it strikes me as true, so I let it rest and Lucia nods happily.

"Again?" she asks.

"Yes, please," I say.

Lucia giggles a bloody gurgle, and I pick her up and we are moving forward. I push the air-conditioning unit out the bedroom window, and we hear it thud down into space as I climb up and push through.

The journey is short this time. Almost as if no time passes and the tunnel was only a couple feet short.

We stand in front of the skin-stitched building again. It is much the same, only the bars on the apartment window are gone, replaced by plywood. Boarded up. The word "condemned" comes to mind. It's a sad word to describe a childhood but perhaps accurate.

I look around at the endless wall of places and find the long aluminum trailer. One window on either side of a beige nightmare. The window facing us is coated in faux-lace curtains marked by small, round cigarette burns. The fabric so synthetic that each little brown burn has grown plastic in texture, a thickly warted bit of cloth that my fingers used to gravitate to when I was stuck inside, wishing to be out. The trailer television—although new and colorful—did not hold the same wonderous appeal. We had more channels, but this TV belonged to him, a new boyfriend, a new shame. This man was named The Neighbor, and he loved his remote control. He held that remote while he slept, while he took a piss, while he yelled and drank and shit.

I was barely ten when The Neighbor moved in, but even before he ditched his next-door shit heap for ours, I had discovered a love of being outdoors fueled by a hatred of the indoors. I far preferred bobcats and mountain lions over the dark of the pseudo-metal box my mother claimed "cozy" so frequently that I knew even she knew she was lying. I always wanted to be outside. So, when he moved in, my mind and body moved out.

I hated monsoon season in that trailer. The rains would pour down full of lightning and thunder. The roof was never strong enough to keep the rain out—each drop sounded like a bullet. The outside world usually knew how to welcome me: Puddles were special things in the desert; the smells that the water kicked up were sweet and full. It was only during the rains in that trailer that I was forced inside. Forced to look out from the dark and finger the burn marks of a man my mother chose over me.

My mother was terrified of the monsoons. She'd once lost her dog to a full arroyo, and she would often repeat, "In my night-mares, my sweet puppy looks like you, Thea." I hated that dog. A dog whose drowning locked me inside with things far more dangerous than rain.

I point to the window, to the curtains. Lucia nods. My girl. So agreeable.

We move through the opening—the trailer door to our left. The sound of that metal door cracking open and clanking shut makes the burrs inside me spike and shift. I'd forgotten that sound. How it was the same sound whether you were coming or going, and how sick it made me feel even when I was pushing out, running into the brighter world. Like the bullets of rain on the roof, it was a noise that sounded like a weapon.

Now, inside the trailer with Lucia, it is brighter than I re-member it ever being. Still dark, but there is an ugly cork lamp on the table and the light from the TV—still the only night-light of my childhood. I sit where I sat as a child, on a stool with my eyes pointed to the blur of the show on the screen—a show he has picked. Sports, most likely, or a crime drama. He loves any show that begins with a dead body. He makes me get close to the screen, watch the actor that's supposed to be dead. He always swears he can see the corpse breathe and calls me stupid for not seeing the same. My mother is in the bedroom, laid crosswise over the full bed, her cheek to the pillow so she faces the wall. Toes hanging over one edge and head the other. She is within reach but far, far away.

The purple hairbrush goes over and over the same spot, lower and lower. He brushes until each brushstroke is so long, it hits the seat of the stool, brushing down and down and down. We pretend this activity is mutual. Hair must be brushed. Bonding should occur. My mother wants me to call him Daddy—she likes this one and thinks it will make him stay longer; perhaps he'll even ask her to marry him and make us a real family—so I refuse to call him anything at all. He tells me his missing finger is due to an alligator bite he got in Florida, even though I know he's never been to Florida and gets compensation from the accident that caused it. He doesn't work anymore. A blown-out knee and a missing digit means he is either in the trailer or by the river.

My mother says that the way he likes to brush my hair is sweet. Says it is something she loves to see us do, even though she never watches. My body cannot be shut tightly enough to prevent exploring fingers, so I watch the TV harder. I learn to hate crime shows where the villains are almost always male and always stupid and always ready to confess.

Lucia looks up at me with her Joker's grin. She wants to make me happy. I see that in her. I wonder how long I missed it. Her eagerness to please. She is so clearly my monster.

"Again?" she asks me, almost shyly.

"Again," I state.

I set Lucia down behind him and she begins to slurp at his ankles, until his body noodles into a limp wave of man.

I should have known he could be easily eaten, I think.

— 126 —

He disappears into the gaping maw of my Lucia, and a space opens inside me where I can suddenly feel pride.

Look at what I made. I smile down at my girl.

His form is visible inside hers. The squirm of him not yet dead, but then he goes quiet, melts inside of her. She absorbs him, growing bigger as she does. Gaining weight and experience. One more goathead shakes loose inside me, dropping down and disappearing. I've finally been able to digest this bit of pain that's been puncturing me each time I breathe in.

"Welcome," Lucia says, and we exit the trailer door.

"Thank you," I answer, and Lucia beams in a way that makes me briefly sad. A couple burrs inside break free, but instead of an extra breath, I feel a bite of guilt.

I push the thought away and kiss the top of her head.

"More," Lucia says, rubbing her tummy.

"Should we stop?" I ask.

She shakes her head vigorously, *No.*

"More," she says again, and does the little hand gesture, tapping fingers to fingers. Sign language for the word "more" that every child learns in kindergarten, and it reminds me of the baby inside of this body. The shape-changing little girl who still wants to make me happy.

Maybe this isn't just about me, I think. The little bite of guilt can be ignored. We are cleaning up the world, making it better for Lucia.

"No more," I say.

The big thing is gone, I think. *Those men who hurt me so badly that I wouldn't let myself remember.* And yet, something worse remains. Something I'm not yet ready to face.

Lucia looks sleepy. We walk through a curtained doorway, and we are back in Lucia's bedroom.

I turn to look at Lucia and see that while she is still herself, a baby girl, she is also me. In some fundamental way, she is me. And I am her. I can see power in her that I don't see in myself, and I wish I were more like her, but at the same time, feel a horrible guilt for the fact that she is so much like me. The selfishness of parenthood hits me. The fact that I thought I could make people and that somehow in making those people I would better understand my own life and purpose. I'd plop them down in this horrible world and help them navigate it in a way that made me feel better even as I knew and know that there is no way around the bad stuff. You go through it no matter what.

∨ ∨

Outside the bedroom door, Dillon is talking to Lilibeth. I hear Sebastian and Jeremy out there too. Trucks clanking against each other, then a quiet arguing.

Dillon is tired on the other side. I can feel his worry. His fatigue. I wonder how long a period has passed for him. Lucia and I have traveled quickly through time, and yet so much has changed. It can't have been too long for him, can it?

I breathe in deeply, and for the first time in decades, it doesn't hurt. The spikes of my insides have gone soft, and my lungs fill to capacity easily and without pain. It feels as if I've been wearing heels all day and, having finally taken them off, realize how fast I can move. How my tendons can lengthen, my knees bend. I could run if I had to. Long strides that my lungs would now allow. It feels good. So good that tears come to my eyes. I did not know I'd been in so much pain. How could I not have known?

"Can you hear us? Do you want me to get the boys out of here?" Lilibeth asks. "I can watch them tonight if you and Dillon want to talk."

I notice she isn't offering to take Lucia. I don't blame her, after what she saw earlier. I wonder if Dillon told her about the chicken too, but then I remember I didn't tell Dillon about Alex Forrest. That secret is still mine and Lucia's.

"We're fine," I say to Dillon and Lilibeth. "You can go home."

All noises on the other side of the door cease.

"You sure?" she asks. "I'd love to take your kiddos off your hands for a bit."

"No," I say. "We just need time as a family. I'll unlock the door, Dillon. But let us come out when we're ready. Give us a minute." I move to the bedroom door and unlock it. No one opens it. Still, I can feel the relief on the other side as he hears the lock release.

"Eat too?" she asks, meaning my husband. Her father.

"No!" I say too sharply, turning back to Lucia. I say again, "No."

I look at Lucia. Then I *see* her. My baby daughter does not look well. The whites of her eyes have gone yellow. Drool slips from the left corner of her shut but gargantuan mouth. Her shoulders look limp, too heavy to hold up.

"What is it, baby?" I ask, and step toward her.

We stand flat-footed, facing each other. Eye to eye. She is green with sick. Her stomach rumbles. She tries to smile to reassure me she is fine but her once-white teeth are coated with grime and gristle. She burps and I smell the sweat of all that shame fighting to either be digested or to come back up her gullet.

"Oh no," I say. "I've taken this too fucking far." All those uglies inside her are too big for her small life. No child should know all that, and I've let her not only know it, but live through it. Eat it whole.

"I okay," she says, but she is beginning to shrink. Wizen down into an old lady, and as she does this, her skin thins, the healthy fat on her body disappears, and it is replaced by sharp little spikes that poke from her insides out. I lift her shirt and see how the goatheads have gone into her torso—how they poke out at her skin, making her look like she's been stung by a thousand bees. They rise, pushing at the skin of her arms. She burps and her neck flushes with the spikes, so big and so many that they pierce through in a few places. Blood trickles down.

"Mama," she says. Her bones are growing spurs, her elbows and knees crackling with them.

"Shit," I say. I try to grab her upper arm, but she screams.

The spikes bite through and into my hand. All this time trying so hard to not be my mother and now I've done just that. Given my baby all my unnamed secrets and my shame.

"I sorry," she whimpers.

"No, baby, it's my fault. What can I do?"

She doesn't know. She wants to be held, so I hold her, then take a step to the door. Two steps and something new will happen. Dillon will save us somehow or she will eat Dillon, or I will know what to do. All I know is that I don't know what to do right now. I don't know what I've done.

But then I hear Sebastian. Sweet Sebastian with his lisp that I hope never goes away, and I remember that Lucia tried to hurt him. To dig his eyeball out. And I wonder how I will protect both my boys *and* my girl.

"Mama," Sebastian wails. He is scared. Lonely. He doesn't understand. How could he?

"I eat him too," Lucia says from behind me.

I hear it neither as a threat nor an offer. It is just what will happen next.

I flash to a world without Sebastian or Jeremy or Dillon and stop myself. Even imagining the pain of that loss is too much.

I let my daughter consume the terror that I spent life trying to distance myself from. I could have stopped it from being passed down.

"Mommy," Lucia says.

"Baby," I say. My voice carries more affection than it ever has for Lucia. The very fact of this makes me feel terrible. Did she do all this to win my love?

She'd seemed happy. Happy in the womb. Happy out of it. Creepy and strangely progressive in growth, but she was a happy kid. All smiles. No need. Still, I know I've been holding back. Watching her, rather than holding her. It's the ones who don't seem to need you that need you the most. It's what I wanted my mother to understand about me. All those years. The more I asked for her help, her love, the more I wished she'd offer it. I closed myself up. Sealed my heart and kept my voice quiet, hoping against hope that she would notice I was gone. She didn't notice. She fed me to the wolves. She loaded me up with secrets that cut at my insides anytime I tried to be bigger, run faster, take in more air.

Have I not done the same? I've taken my baby and made her the villain when she could've been the hero.

"I'll fix it," I say.

She sees me think it as I think it.

Eat me is what I think.

"No," she whimpers.

I step closer.

"Listen to me, baby. You need to swallow me. I'll clean up your insides. I'll get rid of the burrs. You can hurt me if you need to. I'm not important. You're the one who needs to keep living, and if something happens to me while I'm saving you, it will be worth it. None of this is or ever will be your fault."

"No," she says, but I can see her stomach move, the clenching of it like a swirl of man-fists trying to get out.

"You stopped them," I say to her. Tears in my eyes now. "Let me do this."

She shakes her head, *No*, but I am still her mother. She will listen to me.

"I'm medicine," I say. I think I'm right. I hope I'm right. "Take me inside and I'll get rid of the hurt."

She is so small, so recently housed in my body. She perches on the window frame like a big, fat baby bird, and cracks her jaw, opens wide. Her rows of teeth are clogged with remnants— tattered cloth, too-pink bits of skin, tiny flecks of white bone. It's a hellscape of my making.

I bore the villain.

I am the villain.

I walk toward her. I crawl inside. Her teeth scrape my flesh, leave their track marks on my back, my legs. I'll wean us both of all the hate.

⌄ ⌄

I am inside my Lucia just as she was so recently inside of me. My body is intact but impossibly small. It is a warm, pink place if not for the clutter of leftover men that I let her feed on for my sake. My body is safe, but the splintered bones of the dead are blinding in their whiteness, and they poke at her and me like needles. I didn't give my beautiful monster girl a bellyful of goat-heads, but the devoured devils are still ready and willing to assert their manhood. Even the remnant of a dead man enjoys splaying himself about, poking and piercing and taking up all the room. I float in a cavern of calf bones and ribs. Clavicles and molars all sharpened to display their boniest edges. The leftovers of these men are a threat to my sweet Lucia baby's insides. They will hurt her if I leave them as they are. They will do permanent damage.

Motherfuckers. All of you.

I try to raise the anger I know so well in my heart, beat it into my limbs so I can start to solve this problem that I've let my daughter swallow down, but she is so warm. So, so comforting. Her love for me is wonderful, radiating through her and into me. I am almost safe. Is this what I offered her all those months in my womb? Is this why she stayed in there all forty-two weeks? I was so convinced of the monstrousness of my baby boys that my fear of them must have slipped in through the umbilical cord and made each want to come out early—show themselves to convince me they were worthy of love. But, with Lucia, I'd convinced myself she was no monster. My body settled into carrying, and that's what made her emerge fully formed. The warm, quiet space of me allowed her to ready herself and come out hungry. Her true self. I didn't fuck that up, after all.

But I've fucked it up now, using her to clean up my mother's mess.

I remember the feel of that foot brace. My mother would tie

the shoes so tight that the tops of my little feet would be red and raw in the morning. The bar weighted me down. Stuck me in one place, staring at the ceiling. The cracks up there became my friends. I shaped them into faces, finding smiles so I wouldn't be afraid. The bandana tied around my face was yellow, white, navy blue, and so tight that my teeth ground against each other, a dull throbbing that lasted all night long. I'd wake up with a headache that started in my temple and stretched down my neck.

I am suddenly exhausted and half-blinded by the glare of these men, stripped down to bone. If I keep my eyes shut, I could just about go to sleep. Giving up would be nice. My family would be better without me. I could rest a long, long time. Lucia's body is strong. Perhaps, with time, it will heal itself. Perhaps it will eat me. Dissolve this body along with the bones in the healthy acids of her growing body.

I am just about settled in when I hear my mother's voice. Not like in a memory but somewhere just beyond Lucia. Is she in the house? My house? I feel dread. I feel sorrow. I feel defensive. How long have I been inside Lucia? Could my husband have had time to get her? No, he would have taken Lucia, and we've been home for some time now. I know that. I think I know that.

"I've secured a place next door," my mother is saying. "Don't you worry, Dillon. I'm here for the duration."

This does not sound like my mother. My mother does not swoop in to save the day. My anger swells. I reach out and grab a bone, snap it in thirds with my tiny, bare hands, as I listen.

"I'm grateful to you. The kids are too, and Thea will be when she realizes you've stepped up. Thank goodness for you and for Lilibeth," Dillon says.

"Lilibeth," my mother says and snorts. It's her way of implying incompetence without actually saying anything.

Dillon doesn't hear this dig or else chooses to ignore it. Instead, he says, "I just don't understand what's happened. She was in that room with Lucia, then she was gone. Just gone. Lilibeth seems to think she wasn't telling us everything. Like, she was having a harder time than she let on. And there were signs I should have paid more attention to. Ever since Lucia was born . . ."

"That woman knows nothing," my mother snaps at Dillon. "She should mind her own. Thea is fine. She's just having one of her little tantrums.

"Thea has never been happy. Sour and distracted since she was a little girl. I did my best, but she always acted like she knew more than me, then she'd only call me when she was miserable. Weeping over what have you, and I'd try to help but she doesn't want to be helped. Trust me."

Ha! I think. What an amazing twist of a story she's telling about me.

"Can I ask you something?" Dillon says, and I can hear in his voice that he's been fighting the urge. He knows he shouldn't, but he doesn't know *why* he shouldn't. Not yet.

"Of course," she says, as if she is the most generous person in the world.

"Did something happen to her?"

"How do you mean?"

"I don't know. Like, when she was a kid. I've always had this feeling that she was holding something back. Like, if we could just talk more openly, I'd understand more why she is so . . ."

"Angry?"

Fuck you. I aim my thoughts at my mother and snap a few more bones, then realize the rage she is eliciting only makes her kind of right. It makes me smile and burble a little laugh.

"No," Dillon says, careful with his word choice, "not angry. I'd say restrained. Self-conscious."

"Self-conscious! The girl doesn't have a damn ounce of restraint," she says.

"I see her differently than you do. Anyway, I don't mean like that. I mean, like, she thinks I won't love her if she tells me everything."

"Well, good Lord, you won't! I didn't tell my boyfriends everything. Certainly not her father. Secrets keep a marriage healthy."

"Look," he says, "let's drop it. I thought maybe you'd know something."

"She was raised right. I did my best. I can tell you that."

"I didn't mean to imply that you did a bad job. I just . . . I can tell she's lonely. Even with me."

"She's female. That's just how it is."

"Really?" he asks, and I want to shout, but I stay quiet in

Lucia's newfound warmth and instead break a calf bone into tiny, tooth-sized pieces.

"She'll be even lonelier if you find out how crazy she is, and you take her children away from her!"

"What?" Dillon asks. His voice pitching high. "Did you tell her that?"

"No! I mean, of course not. Good Lord. I came out here to help you. You need my help. Who knows when she'll be back. She's selfish."

I need to see what's happening out there, a thing that I don't know is possible, but I do know that it is certainly impossible with all these male bits and bobs cluttering up my daughter's insides. So, I continue to snap them into smaller bits and pieces.

The neighbor kid in the apartment next door to me and my mother had Lincoln Logs. Dark brown sticks of wood with notches that fit to each other. My mother laughed at me when I begged for some, saying, "Those aren't new. Kids have had those since *Little House on the Prairie*," she said, referencing a show I knew well and on which no child had ever played with Lincoln Logs (Nellie was the only villain I never wanted to be). "Trash plays with Lincoln Logs." And when I said, "But we're trash, Mama," she smacked me across the face and told me not to call her Mama anymore.

I adored the way Lincoln Logs fit one to the other. How the stacking together made them more solid than they were apart. I'd long dreamt of building a house for my mother, and suddenly

I'd found the way to do so! She'd be sorry she smacked me. Sorry she made me feel dumb.

When I told her what I was up to, she laughed and laughed. "Dream smaller," my mother said, and so I did.

Until Lucia.

Now my dreams are getting bigger. I take the bones of these murdered men and build a castle. A place for lost children. Children who have seen some shit. Like me. Like Lucia. A place for their dreams and nightmares.

I work slowly. Methodically. My sleepiness has gone away entirely, and it is replaced by awe. The broken bones are still strong; their sharpness lets me carve them into each other. Link them into walls that stretch up and up. I build from the inside. The walls go up all around me. The towers stretch high into the pink of Lucia's stomach, and when it is done and all the bones are gathered and repurposed, I peer out the lowered drawbridge of a front doorway into the healing world of my daughter's insides and out farther through her baby belly button. Her body a snow globe, her belly button the peephole that lets me see out into her world.

I can see her bedroom. A new crib has been installed. The bars whole and unchewed. Parton, Dolly sits on the windowsill. The world is itself again, despite my absence.

How much time has passed? I cannot tell.

The full-length mirror we installed on her wall reveals that Lucia is in her diaper on her bedroom floor. Her body encases me—I am the queen in the castle inside the snow globe of Lucia. I am safe to observe my old house. My old life.

"Don't touch yourself!" my mother shouts. A booming voice from another room. "Why must he do that?"

"Do what, Mema?" Jeremy asks. His voice is the voice he uses when he is nervous. When he knows I am mad but doesn't want me to know he knows.

"Diddle himself!" My mother is talking about little Sebastian. Her voice drips with disgust. "Men are so gross. Remember that."

They aren't all, I want to say. *Don't remember that!* I want to yell.

Lucia crawls into the main living area. I can see my mother is at the sink. She is scrubbing our countertops; concrete of our own careful pouring and she is after them with a chemical cleaner we would never have bought. It makes me wonder if she packed up her whole arsenal of cleaning supplies before coming out to search for her missing daughter.

"Don't you eat another cookie, Jeremy. You'll end up as fat as me," my mother says and sprays and scrubs again.

"You're not fat, Mema," Jeremy whispers.

"You'll be old and ugly one day too. Stave it off as long as you can. That cookie won't do you any favors."

Lucia crawls forward, wrapping just her front teeth around my mother's ankles. My mother shrieks and pulls back. I feel

Lucia as she smiles up at my mother from the floor. All innocence and blue eyes.

"You little devil's shit," my mother mumbles.

Jeremy rushes to gather Lucia. Lucia squirms away. We move in for another taste of my mother's blood but the front door swings open.

Dillon is tired. More tired than I've ever seen him. He has dirt in his crow's-feet—red dirt from the drive. From windows rolled down so he could search for me.

"I took the long way, drove out to the ranch and asked a few workers if they'd seen anything." And by "anything," he means me.

"That's nice," my mother says, not even asking if they had.

"Oh, you shouldn't use that on our countertops," my husband says, seeing the mess she is making, but then Sebastian is running to him, and Dillon is looking at his tiny, shame-faced son. "What's wrong, buddy?"

"Can't keep pants on that child. Thinks his penis is some kind of finger puppet."

"Listen, I appreciate you helping, but we don't shame the kids," my husband says. "Not about their behaviors or their bodies."

I love him so damn much.

"What did I say?" my mother asks. Her palm to her heart as if shocked.

"It's all right," Dillon says. "You've been such a great help to us. We've kept you out here for weeks. We can't possibly keep you here much longer."

I should hear the diplomacy in my husband's voice. The way he is subtly suggesting she leave even though he won't know what to do without help, but all I hear is the part about weeks. I've been gone for weeks? I've been in here building my castle and they've been out there dealing with each other.

"Well, she's not coming back. I'll tell you that much," my mother snaps. "You'll need to figure something out." She slaps down her spray bottle. Her sponge. She has felt his rejection, even masked in kindness, and she is getting sick of helping. The novelty has worn off.

"She'll be back," he says, noticing the tears in Sebastian's and Jeremy's eyes. Lucia crawls me and herself to his ankles so we can be close. He smells like home even from the ground.

"My daughter looks after herself, and if she's decided that means going solo, she isn't coming back. If it isn't selfishness keeping her away, it's death, and dead means dead. No coming back from that."

My husband sighs, heavily. She has not heeded his hint that the children can hear her. Sebastian cries in small hiccups that he buries in Dillon's shirt.

"Lilibeth says she can help," he says.

"Lilibeth? Please. That woman has a whole business to run. Listen, I don't mean to be rude, but I'm the one staying over there with her. I'd know better than you if she's got time to help some poor widower with his kids."

She's been staying with Lilibeth. That makes sense. Renting a room. Dillon has at least had that much distance. Sebastian has been safe from her for a few hours each day.

"Well, I need you tomorrow," Dillon says. "Let's just leave it there for now. That, and I'm for sure grateful for you. Don't know what I would have done." I can hear the sincerity in this. The need of my husband has never been so great, and it makes my heart hurt.

My mother leaves, and my husband picks up Lucia, and we watch my mother hoof it over the hill and down the shallow arroyo to Lilibeth's place. We are all grateful when she disappears inside the house.

I can't stay inside my castle much longer. My daughter's body is beginning to dissolve the bony structure, the turrets melting away like sugar cubes. Dillon, Sebastian, Jeremy, and Lucia crawl into our king bed together. It feels amazing to be in the pile of them. Safe and sound, all in one place.

I need to rest up so I can figure out how to separate from Lucia tomorrow. Free myself and make things right. Her insides are already on their way to healing. I need to be there to help heal the outsides too.

For now, we sleep. A big, purring pile.

PART III

Latch

As my family sleeps, I dream myself born anew. There are no labor pains, no busting out of my daughter's belly. Instead, I crawl upward through the long tunnel of her esophagus—the same path I took to hide inside of her and clear her gut. The tunnel is warm and tight, a regurgitation that I hope she doesn't mind. Ahead there is light, and I move forward. Lucia's jaws open wide, wider, widest to free me. I keep crawling out of the bedroom, out of the house, and into the dark night of the desert. I crawl until day breaks and the heat of the sun bounces off my back.

I wake up far from my family, outside of Lucia, atop my favorite spot of desert—I know where I am without even looking. It's the place I run to for quiet, the same spot where I hope to build a studio, so all parts of me—my love and ambition—can really call this high desert home. Lucia is no longer with me and that's okay. I've left her behind. Whatever comes next is mine to do and mine alone. Lucia is safe with the rest of her family. My family. Spiteless and piled warm, they will wait for me.

The red dust of high desert earth is underneath me, and below that, I can sense the spring, cool and flowing. Life unseen is still life. A pile of partially digested, broken-to-bits bones lies next to me, and I understand that I have thrown them up just before waking. Like the clearing that comes right before the push, my body has emptied everything unnecessary so that I can begin again. The pile reminds me of Lucia's baby teeth piled up on her bedroom floor, which makes me remember the joy of Lucia's warmth all over again, her heartbeat, the purr of my family.

I lie on my side. Not quite fetal, but almost. A New Mexico whiptail lizard sidles up for warmth. His small body a feather against my face.

His blue tail twitches and hits my upper lip. My wrists ache from building the bone structure in a way that I hadn't noticed when I was inside my daughter. My knees too. And my knuckles burn raw in the cold air. I do not want to move to see all the spots that hurt.

"She's the official state reptile," I hear my husband say.

The New Mexico whiptail is a singularly female species, striped with the same blue under its chin that finishes the length of its switch of a tail. Dillon loves those damn lizards, rejoices when winter ends and he catches a glimpse of one sunning on the outside of our house. He calls the children—squeaks in glee and two of them are just now old enough to come running. They name them Leslie and Bernice and Carmine.

"They are plentiful in Albuquerque," the Dillon of my memory says.

"I know," I say. "My mother likes to watch the roadrunners carry them off."

My husband makes a pained face. "They beat them against a rock before they eat them, so they can swallow them more easily."

"I did know that," I say, picturing my mother exclaiming: *Look, Thea, they're readying to gummy another one!*

The first time Dillon brought me up here to his mountain desert, the sun was high and the lizards scattered as we walked. They liked the heat of the path, and Dillon bent down to scoop one up—its tail a short nub. He held it with such grace that I suddenly felt jealous. I wanted to be cupped in his hands like that. Then and forever.

"They are parthenogenetic," he tells me. He's noted the look on my face and mistaken it for interest in the word he's just said rather than in him.

"I don't know what that means," I say shyly, shifting my interest as best as I can.

Dillon is different. He makes me feel like I can be still. Meditative. The anger in me drops away if only for a moment, and without it, there is space inside me. For life. Growth. I feel as vulnerable as the lizard he holds out for me to pet, and I like that feeling. I revel in it.

I reach out one finger to stroke the lizard's ice-blue chin.

"It means the embryo doesn't need a sperm to reproduce."

"Women creating women," I say to him, and he smiles.

"Exactly. Think how powerful that makes you all on your own."

"Where does that leave us?" I asked. "If I don't need you."

"That means you choose me. How powerful is that?"

He felt my love. I gave it to him, and he accepted it. Love itself a virgin birth.

It's hard for me to remember that day, that moment. The realness of it. Its openhearted honesty. I'd forgotten. In between pregnancies and births and the boiling up of old rage, I lost sight of him. Of the me who found him.

I open my eyes and the lizard touches her nose to mine before scurrying away.

My body shivers as the sun pinkens the horizon. Here, outside the womb of my child, I resist the urge to curl my body tighter for warmth. Instead, I roll onto my back, look up to the brightening sky.

Above me, the sky blooms into the pinkie red of a watermelon. A shadow blocks my view. A big, dark spot. Monstrous from the angle of the ground and so unexpected that I shrink into myself—roll tight before I sit up.

"I didn't mean to scare you," says the dark spot.

"I'm not scared," my voice barks back, full of fear.

I hold my hand up over my eyes as if there is a glare keeping me from understanding who I am speaking to.

"It's just me," she says, squatting down.

I see now that it is Lilibeth. My nosy neighbor. My morning walk interrupter. The one who saw Lucia for who she really is. The woman who I now realize has been nothing but kind to me.

"I walk this way at dawn most days. When I see you and the

kiddos, I'm on my second go. Gotta keep your body moving when you reach this age."

"Huh," I say, because I don't know what else to offer.

"You've been gone quite a while," Lilibeth says. "Scared a lot of people. You can't have been out here that whole time, can you?"

"How long?" I manage, but there are layers to my question that go on forever. How long have Sebastian and Jeremy been without their mother? How long has Dillon lost sleep to the not knowing? How long has my mother had to make Lucia smaller than she deserves to be?

"Twenty-one days."

I blink, rapid as a whiptail.

"Remember how I told you it wasn't always the mother's fault?"

"I do," I say.

"Well, sometimes it is. Your mother has been staying with me, and she's a real asshole."

This brings a horselike laugh out of my body. I can see Lilibeth's face well enough to see her mouth twist into a conspiratorial smile.

"I can't squat here too much longer. In fact, you're gonna have to stand and help me unsquat. I think you'd have learned by now that it's rude to ask a woman of my age to get this low in the first place."

"Hey, now," I say. "I've never once asked you to squat down to my level. You just keep doing it."

— 151 —

"True enough," she says. "I've always liked women who like to get down in the dirt from time to time."

I stand quickly and offer my hands. She rises carefully but without too much trouble. Her hands are soft and warm compared to my cold, dry ones. Her knuckles more prominent than mine, as if they've grown with age. The body gnarls. A cruelty I'm sure I will soon discover.

I am barefoot, wearing only black tights and a white T-shirt. My arms goosepimple as my body begins to feel the coolness of morning.

"I'd ask where you've been, but I don't suppose it matters. You're here now."

"That's the second nicest thing you've said to me," I offer.

"What's the first?"

"That my mother is an asshole."

It's her turn to laugh, a great witchy cackle that changes every feeling I've ever had about her to the good.

"Your family misses you desperately. I've tried to help, but well . . . your mother."

"Where is she?"

"Right now? Probably making coffee at my place. Your mother raised you alone?"

I nod my yes.

"She says your father left you guys early."

"I have no memories of him."

"My husband and I wanted more children. I would have welcomed half a dozen at least."

I realize I don't know how many she has, and a blush comes to my cheeks.

"Don't worry. I talk a lot. It's too much to take in. I couldn't have more. Children. My insides are like the high desert. It only blossoms when there's a lot of rain and there is never enough. We got lucky, having the two."

"I'm sorry," I say.

"It's fine. But it is part of why we bought this place out here. We wanted to take care of people. It's why I was so thrilled when you and your husband moved in. Those kids of yours are sweethearts."

"I wish my mother felt that way about them. About us."

She considers this for a while. "You know," she finally says, "a narcissistic parent loves and hates an empathetic child. The empathic child sucks up other people's feelings like a sponge and tries to make everyone feel better. The narcissist loves them most, because that kid will care about them, take care of their every little need. They eventually hate them, because that's also the kid most likely to escape—to realize as an adult that the relationship is not healthy."

"Do you think I'm a narcissist?" My heart is pounding so hard that I'm worried she can hear it.

"No, sorry. No. Your mother. She got stuck somewhere way

back. Maybe when your father left or, more likely, way before that. She stopped growing. She stayed that little girl or young woman, and she hasn't ever made her world any bigger. It's not your job to fix her, but I sense you figured that out long ago. Anyhow, I hope you know that just because that relationship isn't good—isn't growing—it doesn't mean you can't trust the other people who have come into your life. Your kids need you. Dillon too. They see you, and they need you for the right reasons."

"I need them," I say, and it makes a nervous feeling flutter in my stomach. Needing no one is safer.

"Let's head to my place. It's closest, then we can get you back to your family as soon as possible. I can either drive you home or we can call and get them out here," Lilibeth says. "And I know it's selfish, but I love that I get to be the one to deliver you back to them. Is that terrible of me?"

"If it is, I don't mind," I say.

"They will be so happy, and I'd like to witness that moment. Not that any of this is about me, but you've already made my day."

The sky is gaining its heat, and I walk carefully. My bare feet like the cool sand and I know the snakes won't be out until the sun is higher, but I know too that cacti never sleep. The large needles you can see aren't the problem. It's the millions of tiny hairs that follow behind the first, visible prick. The needles that can carpet your foot, invisible but shockingly painful if brushed against a shoe or a sock, so you are never quite certain you are free.

"My mother thinks I'm a monster," I say as we walk, and it surprises me that I've said it even though it doesn't seem to surprise Lilibeth.

"Well, maybe she's right. And maybe being a monster doesn't mean what she thinks it means. Maybe it's a gift and maybe, just maybe, you can use it to show your daughter how to be her best self too."

It's a thought I've never had before.

"She's up already," Lilibeth says. I don't know what she means, but I follow her pointing finger and see my mother out on the porch of Lilibeth's place. She's spotted me.

I brace myself for the worst, and as we step into the stretch of desert that qualifies as Lilibeth's front yard, I look up to see my mother on her porch, coffee cup in hand with her right foot raised high enough to squash the body of a sun-lulled lizard.

˅ ˅

'll give you two a second together," Lilibeth says, as she disappears inside her house.

My mother squints her eyes at me, and for a moment I see something like relief on her face and rethink what I've come to say to her. Was she worried? Did she miss me? It, however, only takes a moment for her to transition into reprimanding me, listing off items finger by held-up finger that prove my negligence as a daughter, a wife, a mother, a woman. I listen, although not attentively, letting her nonsense feed the particular rage monster that I usually starve. I've felt pregnant with this rage baby my whole adult life. She's not small or weak—but she is curled tight in my gut. Hidden inside of me at my own request. What if I let her out? What if I roared as loud as I could? Would the world end? Would my mother keel over dead?

"Where the hell have you been?" she asks as she begins to wrap up her tirade. Spit flies from her lips and droplets fall into her coffee. "And where the hell are your shoes?"

"Hello, Mom," I say, as if it is just another day.

"Typical," my mother says. It's the first line of a skit we've long performed. Next, I am supposed to ask, "What do you mean?" To which she will say the biting comment she has intended from the start. I don't say my line, but she waits a beat, then says hers anyway. "You've never cared about anyone but yourself."

Part of me believes this. The other part of me doesn't care what she thinks.

"Is there more coffee?" I ask.

I've only been in Lilibeth's place a few times. We stand in a common space reserved for guests who rent different private rooms. Light pours in and the smell of coffee is strong and good. Behind that I smell the dried lavender that fills a vase on the long cedar table. I pour myself a cup and sit. The tabletop is smooth, and I run my palms over it before I regrip my coffee mug and take a drink.

"What the hell is wrong with you?" My mother is still standing. Her back is to the kitchen sink. Her fists on hips. She looks like some kind of angry-ass teapot or sugar bowl, and it makes me giggle.

My mother's scowl deepens.

"What's wrong with me?" I ask. "What's wrong with you?"

"Nothing is wrong with me. You're the one who ditched your family."

I take a deep, patient breath and say, "Sit." My mother does not sit. "Now," I add, and she must be as surprised as I am to hear the command in my voice, because she pulls out a chair across the table from me and sits.

I study her face. I notice how her crow's-feet have deepened. Her what-the-fuck line between her eyebrows is a canyon.

"Let's get into it, Mom. Let's talk."

"You have a lot of nerve, young lady. I had to drive out here. Upturn my whole life. And now you are strolling in looking like you've been out camping under the stars. Does your husband know where you are? Where you've been? I don't think he did or does. He was panicked. The poor man. What if I hadn't come out? What do you think would have happened? I tell you what . . ."

"Mom," I say, surprised by my own deep and directed calm. There is a strength in my voice that my mother's presence usually chases away. "I'd like to talk about some things."

"What kind of things?"

"All the things."

"Don't be dramatic."

"I don't intend to be dramatic, but I do have some questions about my childhood, Mom. I'd like some answers from you about things that happened to me as a kid. Most of all, I want to know what *we* are. Where we came from," I say and point to her, then to me. It pains me to group the two of us together even in this small way, but I am her daughter. I came from her body, and if I want to continue on in my own body without living in the shadow of all her fucked-up mistakes, I can't deny any part of where I've been.

She startles. Sits up straight. Looks like I've slapped her, then says, "I have no idea what you're talking about."

"When did you know you were different?"

"Different how? Everyone is different from everyone else. That's a stupid question."

"Mom, focus. Lucia is . . . Well, she's different, and I know I am too. I don't remember everything, but I remember that incident at school. I hurt a little girl . . ."

"That little girl was trouble. She hurt you first."

"Fine. Whatever. I'm not here to argue about that, but I do remember that I also hurt a teacher. A nice woman. Sent her to the hospital, I think, and I have no idea if she came out okay. Did we ever check to make sure she was okay?"

"I honestly have no memory of that," my mother says and waves at the air as if to clear it.

I blink a few times, then try a new angle. "I remember how

you used to make me wear a foot brace to bed and you'd tie my jaw shut with . . ."

"Oh. My. God. Is that what this is about? You had clubfeet. The pediatrician prescribed that contraption. It looked medieval, I know, but it was common practice back . . ."

"Was the bandana tied around my head to fix my clubfeet?"

"Don't be ridiculous."

"Mom. Just stop. Stop telling me I'm crazy when I'm not crazy."

"You said 'crazy,' not me."

"Tell me where we come from. Are you the same? Is that why you tied your jaw shut too?"

"I don't have any idea what you are on about," she says and gets up to go to the sink. She picks up a dry sponge and turns on the water to wet it. She wrings it out, wets it, then wrings it out again more fiercely this time before beginning to wipe down the counters.

"This isn't your house, Mom. You don't have to clean."

She continues to scrub at the marble.

"Mom!"

Sighing and throwing the wet sponge into the sink, she says, "I honestly don't know what you want me to say. You know I was raised by my grandmother. She was a mean old lady, but she kept me alive. I may have had my moments, but I took care of you too. You had what you needed to be happy. It's not my fault you chose not to be."

"Jesus, Mom. At what age do you think I chose to not be happy?"

"You've always been too stubborn and sullen. Since you were a baby."

"You are telling me that I chose to be unhappy for the rest of my life when I was a baby? That's what you're saying?"

"You're twisting my words."

"Am I?" I shout. The rage in me is uncurling, readying to pounce. I pinch the bridge of my nose. Breathe. "Okay, how about this. How about we talk about your boyfriends. Some of them hurt me."

"Don't be ridiculous."

"Mom, I was molested."

"You were not," she says.

"Are you fucking kidding me? You're telling me that what happened didn't happen?

"Let's hit pause and assume for one minute that you were unaware of how they treated me and that there was nothing you could have done differently. If we pretend you were ignorant, then can we talk about it?"

"You watched too much *Oprah* after school. That's what all this is about."

"Stop trying to make me feel like I'm crazy! I'm not crazy. You're trying to brush this off, but I'm not going to let you. Not this time. We're going to fucking talk about it!"

"Well," she says, and puts her hand over her heart as if I've stabbed her there. She plops back into the chair across from me before she speaks again. "Everyone complains about their mother. You do realize that, right? It's a cliché to blame your mother for everything. Did Lilibeth put you up to this with her psychoanalytic bullshit?"

"Bad shit happened to me! Shit I'd never ever let happen to my kids. You let it happen, or worse yet, you used me!"

"I did no such thing," she says and sniffles.

"You used me as a buffer between you and some real shitty men, Mom."

"Family is supposed to look out for each other."

"And that's exactly what I'm saying. That is what family is *supposed* to do. But you didn't protect your child! And you also made me think I was invisible. Weak! I guess I could deal with the fact that you didn't help me, but you didn't let me protect myself."

"Oh, I *did* protect you."

"Are you fucking kidding me?"

"No, I'm not kidding you. And you should know how hard it is to be a mother. More now than ever with Lucia." She says Lucia's name like it is filth to be spit out.

"Lucia is special. Do you hear me? She's not something to be ignored. And no one is going to hurt her. Not like you've hurt me."

"You know what your problem is? You've always been greedy. You want too much. *That's* your problem." This last phrase is an old favorite of hers. A summary statement that can be applied to just about every situation, according to my mother. "I'm always sad, Mom." "*That's* your problem." "I can't get Sebastian to sleep, Mom." "Well now, *that's* your problem!" As if we'd been hunting for just what my problem was for quite some time. Lucky me, she always found it.

"Mom," I say sharply. The anger is stretching to its full height. My jaw hurts. My teeth suddenly feel too big for my mouth. Anger may split my face in half.

"Your daughter is just like you," my mother says with a tone that makes it clear this is not desirable. "Nothing like me."

"You're right. Lucia is nothing like you," I say.

"That's because I keep myself under control. I don't let people see my nasty. You need to wake up and start training her to be a lady."

"And what exactly is a lady?" I ask.

"Well, if you don't know, then I certainly failed. I worked my whole life to keep myself managed. Then I spent another two decades teaching you to keep yourself right. And now you've had your own brood, and if you don't get Lucia under control, she will be a lost cause. You need to curb *it*."

"What exactly is 'it,' Mother?"

"You know exactly what we are. Freaks. Monsters. Me telling you that we are hideous isn't going to change anything." She shoves her coffee cup away from her and it spills heavy drops onto the tabletop. "If you hadn't had a fucking girl, we'd be done with it."

"What should I have done, Mother? Aborted her?"

"Absolutely!"

"You're serious, aren't you?"

"Of course I'm serious, but that ship has sailed, Thea. I made the same mistake with you. I waited too fucking long to make that decision, then there you were, and so it was my responsibility to work even harder to make things right."

"You're saying you should have aborted me?"

"Of course I should have. But I didn't, did I? And here you are. Messing up just like I did, only far worse. Raising a demon baby just like I had to, only you are even more clueless than I was. Thea, you're way out of your depth and you don't even know it. At least I knew I was ill-equipped to raise you. I had to step up my game to get you under control. Are you so fucking naïve that you think, somehow, she won't eat all of you alive the first chance she gets? I raised you to be smarter than this."

"I am nothing like you. Nothing."

"Whatever you say."

"I. Am. Not. You," I say with a growl that surprises me. It is low and fierce and comes from all the acidic parts of me. Somehow it is both familiar and brand-new to me. My mother looks momentarily frightened.

"You have no idea how lucky you are to have Dillon. You've been moping around like you've been robbed of something. All I did was make things right for you. I helped curb your body so it wouldn't change into a monster, and I did so kindly. I never hit

— 163 —

you. I didn't drug you at night to keep you from changing. My grandmother beat the shit out of me. Locked me in closets. Told me I'd go to hell if anyone ever knew what I was."

"What am I, Mother? Tell me."

"You had it good." She pokes a finger at me, ignoring my question. "I had nothing. Just my fucking grandmother who hated me, and a mother who cared more about drugs than me. The fucking island my people come from doesn't even exist anymore, so I gave you what I could. I gave you a home. I tried to find you a father."

Now it's my turn to spill my coffee. The full cup turns over and the brown of it runs a wide puddle that I ignore.

My brain is chasing the implications of each thing she says. I'm beginning to feel confused. Muddled. Like I've lost track of some truth I knew just a minute ago. I can't follow all the nasty little slug trails she's laid down.

"Lucia is made in your image, poor girl. That girl is mean, and you know it. I've seen you look at her like she's a disease. That child is a monster, but it's not too late to fix it. You have the means to stop her from making the same mistakes we made. As long as she never procreates . . ."

"Absolutely not," I say.

"Lucia cannot exist as she is, and you know it. First time I met her, you barely wanted to hold her. You told me she wouldn't latch—you wouldn't either as a baby, come to think of it. Dillon

— 164 —

told me you didn't like nursing her. That you had a choice but are too selfish, I suppose. *That's* your problem."

"Jesus, Mom. That's so fucking mean," I say.

"We can't keep passing down this evil, Thea. You have to stop it. If you want Lucia to live, you have to make other sacrifices on her behalf."

"It's her body, Mom! Not mine. Not yours. You don't have the depth to understand any of what you're suggesting," I say and stand. My voice rises with my body. I put both hands on the table and dare her to rise too. I bite the inside of my cheek and my teeth feel sharp enough to open a hole.

"I never wanted you, but I took care of you anyway! Shouldn't that count for a lot?" she snaps and stands. "Endless sacrifices I've made on your behalf. You would have been ostracized. Killed. Lucia faces the same stakes. If you don't get your shit together and tame her, we will all three of us end up dead. Those men that you say hurt you never questioned your weirdness. The growling you did in your sleep. The ridiculous drooling or all those teeth falling out of your head at once. They understood when I had to strap you into bed. They didn't ask questions or threaten to call social services. They knew better than to ask questions about us. You should be fucking *grateful* for those men. They kept me sane. They fed us. I never told them we are monsters—of course I didn't—but there were signs and they ignored them because I asked them to. For *you*! And if I hadn't done such a good job raising you, protecting you, you wouldn't have Dillon. A good man. A normal man. There is no way he'd have had kids with you if I hadn't kept this family's secrets. You should fucking thank me for this life you have."

I notice two long scars on my mother's face that I haven't seen before. They reach whitely up from the corners of her mouth to the corners of her eyes. She always has too much makeup on or maybe they are visible because the rest of her has gone such an angry red. And something occurs to me. Something that maybe I knew in some way for a long time, so I ask, "What happened to my father?"

"What does it matter, Thea?"

"It matters because I'm asking. Because I want to know!"

"He left! I told you that!"

"No, tell me what happened! What really happened?"

"No."

"No, you won't tell me?"

"No, you don't need to know. It makes no difference what happened to him. He wasn't there for you. I was!"

I stand and smack my hands on the table. I scream so loud that the sound of the words are inhuman. "Just say it!"

My mother either understands the words or finally acknowledges the depth of my rage. The scars on my mother's face open, and her mouth splits so wide that I can see the back of her tongue framed by yellowed rows of too many teeth.

"I ate him," she growls. "Swallowed him whole before he could leave me. You can thank me for that too."

I straighten. Step back in a weak way that clatters my chair to the floor.

"All those fucking men who hurt me and the only one you bothered to stop was my birth father?" I keep my jaw clenched. I can feel the monster in me taking hold.

"I should have eaten you too." Blood drips from the freshly opened cuts on her face, and I wonder how she's kept herself so hidden for so long. Hidden from even me.

"Mama," I growl. "You couldn't fucking eat me if you tried."

"Oh, please. Lucia has shown you more than this. I'm certain of it. I assumed she'd killed you, quite honestly. That she'd done what I should have done the day you were born. The day I saw that I'd passed my monstrousness on to you."

"Fuck you," I say.

"Usually the anger develops over time. Doesn't present until teenage years, but your daughter. Your fucking daughter was born with it. So hungry from the start. A hungry fucking devil like you, but I had the good sense to shut it down with you."

"What the hell does that mean?" I ask.

"I shut you up as soon as I saw what you were capable of. Tied a bandana around your head to keep your jaw shut and your teeth from growing. Hell, I ground them down myself when they needed it!"

And the memory washes over me. I am in her bedroom, on my back on the bed. My feet are secured in two shoes pointing outward.

"Keep your mouth open, Thea!" she is shouting at me.

Tears stream down my face and the pain from trying to keep my jaw open is so great that my face muscles are spasming.

"If you cooperate, this will be over in a jiff."

She has a metal nail file in her hand, and has already been long at work, or at least it feels like a long time. The dust of my shaven teeth clogs the back of my throat. The smell of that white chalk coats my nostrils. Between that and the tears and all the snot that comes with the tears, I can't breathe. I will drown in this mess and my mother will let me. I beg her. I choke out, "Mama, please. Stop, Mama. It hurts."

"I'm almost done," and the metal file is back inside me. It tastes like pennies. It tastes like blood.

My mother sees the look now on my adult face and knows that she's brought a memory back for me. A bad one.

"It was a kindness!" she shouts. "All of it! I swear!"

"Did you ever love me, Mom?" I ask more for the sheer torture of the question than an answer. My mother doesn't know what love is.

"You, you were lucky. My grandmother didn't think about how to support me. She just focused on how to stop me. My first memory is of pain. My grandmother sewing my mouth shut. The stitches burning. And not just once. She did it on repeat every night until she was sure my mouth would stay closed on its own. 'Ladylike,' she called it. I didn't do *that* to you. I fucking should have. Maybe I should do it right now."

"Don't you touch me," I hiss. "Not ever again. And don't come near my family either."

My jaw aches but does not split. I taste blood. I dig my fingernails into the table and the wood gives quickly, as if I'm sinking my nails into the skin of a peach.

"You are nothing without me." Suddenly her mouth is opening. The skin at the corner of her lips cracking. Her big, bloody mouth, and her chin hits the table. Her yellow teeth are old with coffee stains and tobacco. "And I'm all the family you deserve. The only family you need." I watch her rub her belly with her hand as if my father's bones are still in there, as if she lives off his marrow and sinew.

And the thought hits me. Such a simple thought. Something I could have come to understand a long, long time ago: *I am stronger than my mother.* We've both buried who we are—been forced into the light by our own daughters—but I am still young, strong. Unpracticed, true, but whatever mothering instinct my mother is missing is strong in me. My strength, a mother's strength, is unmatchable. It is villainous, and I will eat her alive if she threatens my family.

"You always needed saving," she says, slobbering.

"You let all those men hurt me. You let them use me."

"Don't be naïve," she says. "I did what I had to do to hide

what we really were. Are," she says. Saliva pools on the table. Her loose skin, her weak jaw slops her speech, makes her sound drunk. She can't control who she is. A life of not trying to grow has made her weak; her skin has lost its elasticity.

"You crippled me. Like your grandmother did to you. And you took my father from me for no other reason than he didn't want you."

"He was going to leave us."

"He was going to leave *you!*" I shout, and my mouth bristles with teeth that I never knew were there. I feel how I could happily unhinge my jaw and swallow her. Digest all her fucking bullshit and shit out her splintering bones. It would feel good to hear her scream. To end her with one bite. But I don't want her inside of me anymore. Not in my head and not in my belly.

I think of my Lucia monster, and I know that the power in her has promise. All of it passed down from mother to daughter.

I bend my knees and spring up onto the table like a fucking praying mantis. It is a good feeling. A spry feeling. My mother is the one to step back now, flinching. She tries to shut her big, gaping maw, but it won't quite close. There is too big a rip, too many loose teeth. She uses her hands to hold her jaw up.

I roar into her face. My body all muscle and certainty. Then I see them. My whole family is in the doorway. Dillon looks shocked. Jeremy hides behind his legs and Sebastian cowers behind him. Lucia claps her sweet little hands together in Dillon's arms. She is the only one proud of me—no fear on her face. She reaches for me, but Dillon holds her tight.

My mother looks at me, then at Lucia. Then back at me. She pushes her mouth together, massages her cheekbones enough so that the two flaps of her skin on either side of her face find themselves again and mostly seal shut. Imperfect, but closed enough for talking.

"If you won't deal with your daughter, I will," my mother says, taking a step forward, and I see what she means to do.

"You wouldn't fucking dare."

"Thea?" Dillon asks.

Lucia, still in his arms, wriggles and he sets her down. She moves to a chair and begins to climb onto the seat. Her small hands reach for me on the table. I lock eyes with my mother. Her jaw opening again. She is ready. Her old legs bend in a pounce, but I am on her first. Pushing my body between her and my Lucia.

"No," I growl.

My mother tries anyway. I reach out with my hands turned clawlike and smack her so hard that she reels back onto the floor. I knock teeth loose and they rattle. I step toward her, crush those teeth below the heel of my right foot.

"Get out," I say, and she whimpers. Curls up fetal before gathering herself into a sitting position. I shut my big mouth, soften my face muscles. And turn to Lucia, who has made her own way onto the tabletop. I rush to her, a part of me thinking Dillon will try to save her from me, but he doesn't. He lets her come to me, and I think this must mean he knows she is wrong too. A monster for a monster. I want to cry. The feeling of sorrow almost overpowers me. Almost.

Lucia is warm and strong in my arms and nestles the top of her head into my neck. She smells like baby powder, like milk. A small sob comes out of my throat. The first sob is partly joy. The joy of seeing them all again. The second and the next and the next are because I know I've shown my true self. Lucia may have too. Dillon will take my other two children away from me. He will leave Lucia and me behind.

I can't believe how much I've fucked this up.

I start to say, "I love you," but Dillon speaks first.

"Get out," Dillon says. I muster the energy to beg, but he goes on. "This is not your home. You've done enough damage. Thea doesn't need you anymore. Maybe she never did."

"What?" my mother says. The splits of skin on either side of her face are raw and red and spit bubbles through.

Jeremy puts his hands over Sebastian's eyes to keep him from seeing the gross remnants of it all.

"You said you were here to help, but you did nothing but make us feel horrible and small and dirty," Dillon says to my mother.

"You will not have anything to do with my family, Mother," I say. "Not ever again. Get. The. Fuck. Out."

Lucia claps her tiny hands together again. Such joy for a terribly small monster.

"I've seen Lucia hurt Sebastian," my mother says. "Bit right into him like he was a fucking snack."

"We can handle that. Kids make mistakes. My wife and I can raise our children, don't you doubt that. Right now, we need you gone. That's it."

My mother roars, lifts her jaw with her hands, and lunges at my husband. Her mouth is around his legs before I understand what is happening.

"Don't you fucking dare!" I scream.

I set Lucia on the table and leap across it. My body gone animal. I am fluid in my violence and make it across the surface of the table in one smooth motion. I've never felt so strong, so graceful.

Dillon is screaming, kicking at her throat, her teeth slicing into his knees. I grab him under his arms and pull him free. I lift him from the black hole of my mother and set him down near the boys. He's lost a shoe but is otherwise intact.

I turn back to Mother, my own jaw unlocked, my teeth sharpened into weapons. My body gapes open with an impatient hunger that I've known and misdirected my whole life.

I step forward and wrap my mouth around my mother's head. I swallow her shoulders and her torso. Her scrawny arms stick to her sides as she goes down my gullet. Her skinny legs are weak and give up when I'm at her ankles. I can feel my mother inside me. Swallowed and whole, the shape of her torso visible through mine, her feet pointed daintily, pushing out at my neck. I lumber outside, then gallop to her car. The boys gasp, but the sound has a tinge of glee in it, like when they see a backhoe in operation and we have to stop and admire it for a while. My body a whole new miraculous thing that moves quickly across Lilibeth's yard to the driveway with ease. I feel beautiful. I am beautiful.

I reach my mother's car and tilt my head to the sun-bright sky. I gargle, then hock her up. She lies on the sand between me and her car, gasping. She looks like a worm washed upward from Dillon's garden during a summer monsoon. She wriggles and thrashes. I do not help her. I stand where I am. I let my mouth and body ease back into the shape of a woman's.

"Go," I say, my growl the last sign of my tremendous monstrousness.

"You can't do this to me. I'm your mother," she wails and thrashes wetly.

"Now," I say and turn my back on her. I begin the walk back to my family.

Dillon has Lucia in his arms and Sebastian and Jeremy stand beside him on the porch. Even Lilibeth is there, and I know suddenly that she too will long be part of what I picture when I picture family, whether I'm still with them or not. The sadness comes back. It washes over me. The learned grief of being other when all I want is to be a part of them.

We face each other—me and my family—until we hear my mother's car start. Its axle bumps up against the boulder buried in the ground near our property.

"Breathe, Mama," Lucia says as Dillon steps up to place her in my arms.

I let out a big bunch of air I didn't know I was holding. I kiss Lucia's soft, sealed cheek.

"We'll go," I say to Dillon.

Lucia and I can start again somewhere else. Maybe leave New Mexico. A new state, a new start. I can help Lucia. I'll figure out how to teach her to express herself without doing harm.

"Go?" Dillon says. "You just got back."

I look at him. I keep my eyes on his. I let him look at me too. We are all quiet. All five of us studying each other.

"We'll hurt you," I say.

"So? Everyone hurts each other. The good stuff certainly outweighs the bad."

"You don't understand. I'm just like my mother. Lucia is like me. We might hurt you. The boys."

"You won't."

I start to gather the words to tell him he is wrong. I am dangerous. He does not know me. He does not know his own daughter. Our other children aren't safe around us. We don't deserve family. I don't even deserve Lucia.

"I've done terrible things." I say "I" on purpose because I made Lucia fix my problems. With time, I can undo that damage. Surely I can. And by leaving, Sebastian and Jeremy will never have to know which parts of them are me. They can be like their father and ease into the world as they are.

"We've all done things," Dillon says. "I saw who you were when I met you."

I laugh and say, "I'll let you keep thinking that." I kiss his cheek. "And I suppose I didn't quite know what I was getting into with you either. But I pick you, Dillon. This is our chance to teach our children how to grow into their true selves."

"I love you, Thea."

"All the broken and roaring bits?"

"Every last one."

My husband's arms are strong. Bones full of marrow and covered in tendons and muscles, striped with veins, and finished off with skin. He smells like woodsmoke and coffee. He smells like my children. Their small bodies are latched onto ours and ours to theirs, fastened into a family.

Acknowledgments

As always, I am grateful for my family, who continues to support me in this adventure, talking through my crazy, grim ideas as if they all have merit. For my little brother, who loved to play with "frucks" when he was a kid, and to his sweet family, including two boys whose imaginations are bigger than mine will ever be. Thank you to the Wallis crew and to Yellow Springs as a whole— I'm so glad to be raised by you.

Thank you to Mary Carroll Moore, my writing partner and friend. It's hard for me to think of being on this writing journey without you! Speaking of great writer friends, thank you to Katrina Kittle for staying in this with me for so damn long. I am so lucky to have so many dear friends—some writers and some not—who supported me throughout the writing of this book: Eli Nettles, Michael Himelfarb, Laura Matter, and Mandy Minichiello, as well as Shelbi Stoerner and the early-morning workout crew. Thank you too to Rae Ying-Ling for helping me figure out where I come from. And I am, of course, grateful for the fierce support of Maria Whelan and Kimberly Witherspoon at Inkwell.

ACKNOWLEDGMENTS

Daphne Durham and Aranya Jain, thank you for making the best parts of this book surface.

Finally, I am grateful to all my students over the years who have let me be a part of either their raising or the raising of their own works of literature. It is a privilege to know you and an honor to have earned even a small portion of your trust.

Photo by Li Canorro

Rachel Eve Moulton earned her BA from Antioch College and her MFA from Emerson College. Her debut novel, *Tinfoil Butterfly*, was long-listed for the Center for Fiction First Novel Prize and nominated for both a Shirley Jackson Award and a Bram Stoker. Her second novel, *The Insatiable Volt Sisters*, was named as one of the top ten horror novels of 2023 by the *New York Times Book Review*. She's spent most of her life as an educator, writer, and editor. She lives with her husband and two daughters in the mountains east of Albuquerque.

VISIT RACHEL EVE MOULTON ONLINE

RachelEveMoulton.com

 RachelEveMoulton

 ChellMoulton